Penguin Crime Fiction
Editor: Julian Symons
Hazell and the Three-Card Trick

DEC 1

$1·9

P. B. Yuill is the pseudonym of Gordon Williams and Terry
Venables. Gordon Williams is the author of several novels,
including *Big Morning Blues*, *Walk Don't Walk*, *The Siege of
Trencher's Farm* (filmed as *Straw Dogs*) and *From Scenes Like
These* (for which he was a Booker Prize runner-up). He was
born in Paisley and spent several years as a journalist. Terry
Venables has the unique distinction of having been capped by
England at every level in football, from schoolboy to full
international, no other professional having played for the
England amateur team. He joined Chelsea at the age of
fifteen and has also played for Spurs, Queens Park Rangers, and
Crystal Palace, the club he is now managing.

The two authors met in the 1960s when Terry Venables was
captain of Chelsea and Gordon Williams, then a freelance
journalist, was asked to run the team's business activities.
Their first joint venture was a soccer novel, *They Used to Play
on Grass*. They say that the gimmicky publicity accorded to
their somewhat unlikely writing partnership made them choose
the name P. B. Yuill when they decided to write detective
stories, both of them having an uncle of that name.

Their thrillers are built around the London private detective
James Hazell, the first being *Hazell Plays Solomon* (Penguin;
1976). *Hazell and the Menacing Jester* is being published
simultaneously with this volume. Thames Television are
currently filming a 13-part series centred on James Hazell,
due to be released later in 1977.

D0992722

P. B. Yuill

Hazell and the
Three-Card Trick

Penguin Books

Penguin Books Ltd, Harmondsworth,
Middlesex, England
Penguin Books, 625 Madison Avenue,
New York, New York 10022, U.S.A.
Penguin Books Australia Ltd, Ringwood,
Victoria, Australia
Penguin Books Canada Ltd, 2801 John Street,
Markham, Ontario, Canada L3R 1B4
Penguin Books (N.Z.) Ltd, 182–190 Wairau Road,
Auckland 10, New Zealand

First published by Macmillan 1975
Published in Penguin Books 1977
Reprinted 1978

Copyright © P. B. Yuill, 1975
All rights reserved

Made and printed in Great Britain by
Hazell Watson & Viney Ltd, Aylesbury, Bucks
Set in Monotype Times

Chapter One

We drove along Oxford Street in silence, the sad widow and I. It was one of those damp February afternoons when the sky is like dirty dishwater and brick walls are sweating old grease.

The lights stopped us at Tottenham Court Road, facing the Centre Point skyscraper. A conga line of chanting Hare Krishners was jigging happily along the northside kerb but Mrs Spencer was busy looking across at the underground entrance.

It was down there in the Oxo cube that Mr Spencer had hit the rails. I hoped she wasn't going to weep.

She was around fifty, a pale-faced brunette going grey about the wisps. She had moles on her knobbly chin, the kind that grow little tufts of hair. She was wearing a heavy green coat, a brown velvet hat with a black band, and those furry bootees that went out with gas masks and running-boards.

Her left cheek had a slight twitch and the rest of her boatrace had two expressions – a mournful stare that made your average bloodhound seem like Woody Woodpecker, and a brave smile, the kind that's supposed to touch your heart.

As far as I was concerned the dreary widow had only one touching feature.

How much of it I could touch I was still trying to find out. She kept saying she was broke but they always do. I knew there was a mite there somewhere.

The lights changed and I went over into New Oxford Street, right under the useless empty road under the useless empty skyscraper, back into Charing Cross Road and then left into Oxford Street again, this time facing west.

'According to Mrs Locke they usually set up their pitch between here and Oxford Circus,' I said.

'You'd keep driving up and down till you saw them, I suppose,' she said, in her sad voice. She had a sad voice and a firm voice. The firm voice was pretty sad, too, but it was louder.

'No, it has to be done on foot,' I said.

'But it would be much easier in a car,' she said, in the firm voice.

'Easier on the legs, yeah.'

I turned left into Soho Street and spent ten minutes chasing my own exhaust pipe round Soho Square before I got a meter.

'By the time I parked they'd be off,' I said, switching off the engine. 'Having it away on their toes is what these hounds do best.'

She nodded slowly.

'What would you actually do?'

'If I tried to chat 'em up in the street they'd very likely give the slip. These geezers could dodge diphtheria. No, I'd follow one of them home, get him pinned down to an address.'

She sighed. We both stared out the windscreen. I felt tired. Finding clients to employ you is the hard part of this racket. And finding them again when you want paid. The sleuthing in the middle is usually easy enough.

'How long would it take?' she asked.

'Dunno. A week. Or I might spot 'em first day out. If they were predictable even the law might trip over them.'

'Why – don't the police try to catch them?'

'Not that you'd notice.'

'Why ever not?'

'If you're cynical you believe the rumours. They say it's lack of men.'

'Honestly – you can't trust anybody these days. How much would you charge me?'

'Twenty-five pounds a day.' I'd told her this five times already.

'Oh yes.' She bit the fingertips of her glove. A Rolls stopped to see if we were leaving the meter. The driver was a kid in his twenties, long hair, sheepskin jacket woolly side out. It wasn't an old Rolls either. Some pop maniac I shouldn't wonder. I shook my head at him. He went off on another lap of the square. Why didn't I have a trade like that?

'I'm sorry to sound so dithery, Mr Hazell, but it's such a lot of money to me.'

'Yeah and that's only the start.'

'What do you mean?'

I was going to tell her the odds against getting fly boys from a three-card trick outfit to admit they'd helped mangle her husband under a tube train but I tried to put it more tactfully.

'Even if I get hold of one of these blokes I can't guarantee anything. Short of bunging them a fair bundle I don't see any way you'll get them into that coroner's court.'

'I wouldn't be in trouble for bribing witnesses, would I?'

'We'd call it a reward for information.'

'How much would they – I mean –'

'We could offer them a couple of hundred and see how that grabs 'em.'

She drew in a sharp hiss. She did a lot of that, between clenched teeth. I lit one of my duty-free Rothmans. She gave the fag a sour look. Out of consideration for her recent bereavement I rolled my window down an inch.

'How much is the insurance worth?' I asked.

'Insurance?' She frowned. 'Oh – you mean Arthur's policies? You know – I'd quite forgotten all about *them*. Not that they're worth much – Arthur was hopeless with money.'

'If it's a suicide verdict the insurance company won't pay out,' I said, blowing smoke at the open slit of window.

'You don't think I'm doing this for the insurance money! I can assure you, Mister Hazell –'

'If you'll tell me what the insurance is worth we can work out how much you can afford.'

A moment's silence – out of reverence for the dear departed's soul no doubt. Yeah, sole beneficiary.

'There was a big policy but Arthur cashed it in some years ago. I think there are two small policies – as far as I can remember they're for about five thousand each, I haven't –'

'So we're talking about ten grand. Worth investing a few

quid to make sure you collect, isn't it? There's no risk – you don't pay them till they've been to court and done the needful. The only money you're risking is my twenty-five a day. Still –'

Her head swung round sharply.

'Yes?'

'Tell you what I'll do. They want a lot of rent in advance for that office of Fitch's – you pay me a hundred now and I'll only charge you twenty a day.'

Wasn't that noble?

'But you said it might only take one day!'

I turned my head away in case the sight of my chompers might scare her.

'If I nab 'em first day out I won't tell you about it till the end of the week,' I said grimly, 'then you won't know I diddled you out of three days' money.'

'There's no need to be sarcastic,' she said, in the firm voice. 'In my position I have to be extremely careful. It's not easy, when you've been married for thirty-three years to a wonderful man who took care of everything.'

'Yeah, must be tough.'

I thought he was hopeless about money?

That was before, wasn't it?

She got a plastic folder out of her handbag and made out a cheque for one ton to James Hazell.

I won't say I snatched it out of her hand but it was a near thing for two of her fingers. That hundred was going to put me in business.

'I'm sure you'll do your best for me,' she said, no doubt trying to reassure herself, 'after all, you got a lot further with Mrs Locke than the police did.'

That was truer than she knew.

Short of marrying Mrs Locke, the reluctant witness, there was no further I could have gone.

'I'll walk with you to Oxford Circus,' I said, putting the cheque in the lining pocket of my shorty suede coat.

As I was locking the wagon one of Soho Square's resident

wine-connoisseurs lurched up with a yellow bucket on his right arm.

'Wash yer car forra coupla bob, guv,' he announced.

'Piss off,' I said.

He rolled away muttering revenge. I bunged three bob in the meter. Mrs Spencer looked at me with expression number one. It was a cert a church-goer like her didn't go much on piss offs but on the other hand it was probably a comfort to know she'd hired a linguist.

We went into Carlisle Street, right at the pizza place into Dean Street and left into Fareham Street. Soho was its usual alluring self, if you find secondhand dentures exotic, and Fareham Street was a gem. It's an alley running between Dean Street and Great Chapel Street. Neither of them are winning civic awards but Fareham Street? It's about thirty yards long. There's a dreary-looking pub on the corner and it's the beauty spot.

It all happened very quickly, just one of those everyday incidents they always remember to forget in the jolly tourist propaganda.

Three men had been passing on the narrow pavement and one of them hit another in the face for bumping him.

We were just in time to see his left hook. It wouldn't have tickled Mohammed but it broke the bloke's specs. As quickly as if they'd been under starter's orders big drops of dark blood came bubbling out of his nose.

The other geezer, a youngish office-type to look at, walked away with his mate, in no great panic.

'I never even touched him,' the middle-aged man moaned as we reached him. Blood rained on the pavement. Hard lines on him but Fareham Street was brightened up a hundred per cent.

He looked near to tears. I gave him my handkerchief. Mrs Spencer could only stare. It isn't the kind of entertainment they get a lot of, out there in the Ruislip hydrangea belt.

I picked up the broken bits of his lens. He put them in his wallet. He kept asking why anybody would want to clobber him for no reason. He sounded like the kind of patriot who gives teenagers the Dunkirk peptalk. I said there were a lot of weirdos about these days. I was just going to tell him I could remember when men still gave up their seats in the tube to ladies when he grabbed my arm.

'You were witnesses – we'll keep them in sight until we spot a constable – they can't have gone very far –'

'Sorry mate, we're busy.'

'Animals like that shouldn't get away with it,' he whined.

'It's what living in London is all about,' I said. That was the *Evening Standard*'s advertising slogan that year. He didn't see the humour.

'It's your duty,' he snapped.

Mrs Spencer surprised me.

'You haven't even said thank you for this gentleman's hankie,' she snapped back.

'Keep the bleeding hankie,' I said before they could start one of those middle-class snarling matches. Nobody acknowledged the pun. We walked away. 'Makes you wonder what the country's coming to, don't it?' I remarked, curious about this new side to her.

'I don't like men who won't stand up for themselves,' she said, in the firm voice.

Yeah, I thought, we know where standing up for himself got your husband, don't we? Dead on the live rail. I didn't say this to her being tactful – and worried she might cancel the cheque.

We went up Oxford Street on the south side. A fat lady with a clipboard wanted us to help with market research into small cigars. A Hare Krishner, usual model, shaven head with a pig-tail, pink robe, football socks, gym slippers and American accent, tried to flog us the divine truth pamphlet. A young chap with a clipboard wanted us to help with market research into equity bonds linked with life assurance. More marketing than research, actually, as he was standing outside the life assurance offices at the time.

Nearer Oxford Circus all the young hustlers were throwing covers over their mobile racks of t-shirts and cheap beads and plastic umbrellas to dodge the beat copper.

A sad-faced geezer with a pavement spread of furry animals, the wind-up kind that jump around, couldn't hide his merchandise but the copper only gave him a brotherly smile and passed by.

It wasn't his turn to be nicked. They do it on a rota basis. There aren't enough men in the force to grab all the spielers flogging junk in Oxford Street.

The ones without licences, I mean.

At the entrance to Oxford Circus station Mrs Spencer put her hand on my arm and looked up at me.

'You will do your best for me, won't you?' she said, in the sad voice coupled with the touching smile.

'I'll give you a ring soon as there's something to report.'

She disappeared down the stairs. I hung about for a few moments in case she doubled back to check on me.

She didn't. I told myself not to get a complex about her. She was right to be careful about her money.

I turned back into the crowds. Did you know that the old name for Oxford Street was The Stony-Hearted Stepmother? My Dad told me. It was also the route the gallows carts used to take from Newgate Prison to Tyburn, now Marble Arch.

It's still stony-hearted. Mugs get skinned there on the hour. The pavements are very hard. By the time I reached Tottenham Court Road my dodgy ankle was hurting something diabolical.

I gritted my teeth Dunkirk-style. For a hundred quid I had ankles to spare. Her cheque was going to make me a Mayfair man. Really I should have been whistling, considering the fluke that had brought Mrs Spencer's money into my life but I couldn't help wondering what had gone wrong.

Only the week before I'd been poncing round the Mediterranean on a sunshine cruise, being paid good steady greengages to rub shoulders with glamorous actresses and vulgar millionaires.

Still, what the hell.

Live now, pain later.

Chapter Two

When I parked the Stag that freezing January morning about three weeks before I was planning to tell Dot Wilmington I needed a break from the muck and bullet line.

I'd been with her so-called business consultancy for about eighteen months. A lot of the work was with industrial firms, factory jobs, missing stock, that sort of thing. Being an under-cover man isn't so wonderful if it's grimy overalls you're under.

When I came in out of the little mews and up the stairs to Dot's room she was unscrewing the cap of her flat brandy flask for her ten o'clock shot of three-star and dry.

'You're late, don't sit, we're going out,' she croaked, throwing over the thimble-sized tot. 'Is your passport up-to-date? God help you if it isn't.'

'Why, he get passports cheap, does he?' I growled. It was just her morning manner but the crack of a whip is a sound I've never gone a lot on as it happens.

She put the flask in her handbag and pulled on her sheep-skin coat, a small, dumpy woman with washed-out fair hair and a podgy face.

'It's all right about his passport,' she shouted up the carpeted stairs to the open door of Maureen Pegg's room. Pegg was Dot's office manager and 'friend'. She was a bitch. She was always querying my mileage claims and asking me for time-sheets and all that crap.

'What about that man Jago?' she shouted back down the stairs.

'Fix up a meeting here,' Dot bawled. I was always surprised those two bothered to use the phone for local calls. 'I'm not dragging myself all the way to bloody Croydon in this weather.'

'He won't like it.'

'Sod him.'

We went out into the cobbled mews and got into the navy-blue Stag. She told me to drive to Lombard Street in the City. I grunted. There's only one time I like being under a woman.

On the other hand I liked my seventy-five quid a week. I told myself to forget she was a woman. She was just a boss, the same as all bosses, a devout believer in harder graft, longer hours and one-sided loyalty.

'You've been moaning about dirty work,' she said as I was turning right into Kensington High Street, 'now you can be your normal flashy self, thanks to Coulter. He was fixed up for this cruise but he's gone down with gastric flu, silly bugger. The really successful people never get ill, do they?'

'Yeah? What do you mean, cruise?'

'How much do you know about the running of casinos?'

'Mum took me to bingo once.'

'Never mind, they'll show you the basics. We're going to see a Mr Barclay in Lombard Street. He's managing director of a subsidiary company that handles the ships' casinos for R. K. Brown Cruises Limited. They run a whole fleet. Not Monte Carlo stuff, of course, it's the new classless cruise operation – if you've got eight hundred quid for a ticket they don't care if you pick your nose at the captain's table. The captain's the one who's trimming his toenails with the razor-blade.'

'So?'

'Last two trips out this boat had a fifteen per cent drop in the casino take. The computer spotted it where nobody else did and now they're wetting their knickers in case some clever dick's twigged how to beat their security system. It's probably only a computer error, useless bloody things, but you get a sunshine cruise out of it.'

'Where to?'

'The Greek Islands. Eighteen days. All the randy Blackpool landladies you can handle.'

'I'd better buy some suave gear – on expenses, of course,' I said, beginning to brighten up.

'You won't have time – you're on the Southampton train that leaves Waterloo at half-past six.'

'Tonight? Shit!'

'Had one of your little darlings lined up, did you? What age are you – thirty-three? About time you fixed yourself up with something permanent, isn't it?'

'I'm thirty-four. I tried that permanent caper once before, remember?'

'Old age can be very lonely you know?'

'Old age? Leave me out!'

Just before nine that night I was on the pier at Southampton looking up the floodlit cliff-face of the SS *Apollo* and wishing I hadn't bothered to see *The Poseidon Adventure*.

Eventually I got hold of an Irish steward who took me to the purser's office, where they had me on the list as a trainee assistant manager, recreation. Paddy then took me along a few miles of corridors and stairs to a cabin that was just big enough to swing a cat in, if you like cats cheek-to-cheek.

I was still unpacking when Paddy came back with a lofty young toff in a brown corduroy suit and a denim cap.

We introduced ourselves. His name was Kevin Barclay. He was also doing his first trip as a casino trainee.

'I say,' he drawled looking into the cabin, 'quite makes one feel one's in the cabin scene from *A Night at the Opera*.'

I didn't understand.

'The what?'

Paddy wriggled past me and brought down another folding bunk.

'You know – the Marx Brothers' film?'

'Oh. Never saw it. I'm a Laurel and Hardy fan meself,' I said.

'Oh? Really? One always imagines Laurel and Hardy fans as typical *Daily Mirror* readers.'

'Yeah? That's funny, I am a *Daily Mirror* reader, ain't I? So was Liberace, wun he?'

'I say – no offence intended, old boy, I should hate to think one was getting off on the wrong foot.'

'Never mind one, squire – wot about two an' three?'

He examined me with a well-bred frown. I could see we were in for a ball.

Actually he wasn't a bad nut, Kevin, once you sussed that *one* meant you or me. It was no coincidence his name was Barclay. Mr Barclay in Lombard Street was his Dad.

Kevin was working up the hard way, two months' solid slog in every department and a seat on the board as a reward for two years' lifelong devotion.

Still, being a toff meant he always wore clean socks, which was a blessing.

That cabin was so small I was usually nearer his feet than he was.

Second night out I was in the casino about nine o'clock, or bells. With dinner still being served the tables were fairly quiet.

I stopped near a roulette, wondering where I'd seen that face before. She was about twenty-six, a very attractive sort with a great shape, a dazzling smile and long black hair. She was getting advice from a short, silver-haired geezer. His silver hair was an expensive wig and his mohair suit wasn't shmutter either.

He was about fifty. From snatches of his patter I had him down as a cockney who'd found one of the ways to get rich without the handicap of proper English. He didn't half fancy his chances with the black-haired richard.

You know what they say, money won't buy back your youth but it can get you across the generation gap.

She was leaning forward to place her chips when she caught my eye. She caught it enjoying the sight of what was trying to fall out of her white wool dress.

I mouthed the word *black* but she put her chips on red. I shook my head. The ball came round in sixteen red. She pouted at me as the stick shoved over her winnings.

'Yeah luv, I'll keep yer seat for yer,' said Silver Wig as she pushed back her chair.

He caught my eye and made a pained face to let me know exactly what was on his mind.

I didn't pump my arm in agreement. In the classless cruise business somebody has to keep up the tone.

I did a slow circuit of the big room. It had two roulettes, a chemmy table and a blackjack table. When I saw the black-haired party come out of the ladies' room and go up to the bar I came over thirsty all of a sudden.

'Next time you want to take my advice,' I said, sliding in beside her, 'you were lucky that time, believe me – and I'm a wizard of roulette.'

'You're not, you work here,' she said.

'They only hired me to cut their losses. Care for a drink?'

'Thank you. I'll have a sweet martini, please. What's your name?'

'James, but my friends call me James.'

'I'm Stephanie Parmenter.' She giggled, watching my face. I didn't react. That made her a bit impatient. 'I'm on the television a lot.' Quick as a flash I said:

'Wouldn't you be better on the sofa?'

She frowned.

That was why her boatrace was familiar, from the vision. She had black hair and a full mouth so they were always casting her as the low-cut peasant wench or the fun-loving Italian countess who's really a ruthless communist agent.

I saw Silver Wig clocking us busily from his seat at the roulette and decided I hadn't time for the subtle approach. There weren't many females under fifty on that boat and I wasn't going to take turns in the barrel.

'It's no good you asking me what my cabin number is,' I murmured confidentially, 'we're not allowed to entertain lady passengers in our hammocks.'

She stared at me, wide-eyed.

'I didn't ask for your cabin number!'

'You didn't? Oh. Why is it I've always got to do the asking?'

She hesitated. Then she laughed. Silver Wig came bouncing

towards us, cocky little berk. He had short legs, small feet. I raised my voice:

'I'll have the steward bring Moddom a hot-water bottle if Moddom will give me her cabin number.'

She raised her left eyebrow.

'Cabin seventy-one, James.'

She couldn't act off-stage either but I was in business.

She left the casino about half-past ten, giving me a cool look over the tables. I wasn't due off duty till one a.m. but I asked Kevin to cover for me. If Eric Atkin the casino manager asked for me would he say I'd gone to my cabin to take some seasick pills?

It didn't take five minutes in Stephanie Parmenter's cabin for me to get the wool dress off her and for her television cleavage to go on the missing list. It was all an illusion of the bra-maker's art. Call me a naïve sentimental fool but I felt cheated. Half of these actresses are only up there because of their big bells and if they don't really have big bristols why the hell are we bothering to watch them?

Not that she noticed any disappointment on my part. She had a fine time. She kept her eyes shut most of it, probably to help her remember what her own face looked like.

I think she was a bit insecure, deep down, for afterwards she wanted to hear me saying how marvellous and wonderful and fantastic it had been.

'All right, I'll tell you straight,' I said, stroking her black hair, 'this is the best memory I have of this cruise.'

'Memory? But it's only just happened!'

'Amazing how time flies, innit?'

Then she decided I was joking.

'I can't tell when you're kidding,' she said, 'you never smile.'

'Neither would you if you didn't have any teeth,' I said, putting my hand over my mouth. She stared in disgust. Then she remembered I was wearing teeth when she last looked.

'There you go again,' she complained.

I got off the bed and pulled on my y-fronts, wondering if I'd ever meet a woman I could live with for the rest of my life.

'I'm not really so sure this was a good idea,' she said in a little girl's huffy voice, waiting for me to gasp – Oh no, Precious One, you have shown me Heaven.

'Where's the harm?' I shrugged.

She pouted and got hold of my arm and reproached me with a soulful look, the third bit of acting she knew. I gave her a kiss and stroked her black hair and she said next time she would make it truly wonderful for me as well.

'You're beautiful,' I murmured.

In a boatload of widows and grannies she was worth a bit of effort.

'Tummy feeling better?' Kevin drawled when I strolled into the casino, now a lot busier.

'I took the pills. Anything doing?'

'Not really.' He tapped my arm and looked across the room at the blackjack table. 'I say, she's quite a dish, isn't she? The girl dealer with the lovely shuffle and the ace pair up her jumper. She's Australian, you know. I got a chance to survey her attributes while that loud little vulgarian with the silver hair was having his lucky streak – she's luscious, isn't she?'

'You mean that little cockney geezer with the wig?'

'He's at the bar now. How can you tell it's a wig? Most wigs look like bad thatching jobs to me, always the wrong colour and peeling at the edges.'

'I helped him wash it yesterday, he was on soap and I worked the mangle. Of course it's a wig. How much did he win?'

'Close on five hundred smackers. He picks his teeth, you know, breaks matches and uses the jagged ends!'

'How ghastly for one. You know his name?'

'Ah! You'll never believe it – Simon Coddington! Isn't that too much? I'll bet you a fiver it's really Cohen.'

'How did he manage to win so much?'

'He got good cards I suppose.'

'Is that as technical as you get?'

18

I drifted towards the Australian girl's table. Her name was Jennifer Carmichael. In her file at Lombard Street it had said she was twenty-eight, single, an experienced dealer and croupier who'd been working London casinos for four years before joining R. K. Brown Cruises. The personnel card had no soul. She was the business. She had auburn hair and looked younger than twenty-eight. She looked as if she'd spent her whole life in the sun by a pool.

I waited for a lull.

'So how's trade, cobber?' I said to her.

'Piss off, pommy bastard,' she smiled.

'Shoot through, you mean, donchyer? I was feeling a bit crook a moment ago. I can't remember any more Australian spiel.'

'Thank Christ for that. You see that little fella winning four hundred and eight quid? Wow.'

'Fluke was it?'

'He's no mug. Soon as he saw the chance of a five-carder he was in like Flynn. Next hand he gets a twenty-one. Third hand he draws two aces, splits them and comes up with another five-carder. Still, I'll get it all back off him before this tub sees Southampton again.'

'Unless he's a pro.'

'You don't get pros on this kind of boat. Only on this side of the table.'

'Maybe you could teach me a few card tricks. Why don't I buy you a drink when you pack up – sport?'

'I don't drink – sport.'

She gave a big white smile to a middle-aged foursome who were thinking maybe a little flutter would be good for a giggle. She had auburn hair and dark brown eyes that smiled a lot, until she started dealing.

'Okay – how about a game of deck tennis?' I said quietly.

'Sorry, I sleep most of the day.'

'Me, too! That's handy, innit?'

'Piss off – sport,' she murmured, smiling brilliantly at the middle-aged punters as they wriggled on to their stools.

It wasn't much to go on but this little cockney geezer's win was the only unusual thing that had happened so I decided to keep tabs on him and Jennifer Carmichael. Reckoning that a boss's son wasn't liable to be involved in a fiddle I asked Kevin to keep an eye on her while I was off-duty. I told him I had an idea she might not be smart enough to spot if there was a card-sharp among the passengers. He said it would be a pleasure. I told him not to get too steamed up over her as I had plans there myself.

He said may the better man win.

Only neither of us got a chance to try stick or bust with the luscious girl dealer from Down Under. She jumped ship at Gibraltar. She was not missed until the last crew check before sailing. It was too late to search the Rock.

I shot off a cable to Dot.

A few hours into the Med a steward reported that one of the passengers had not returned to his cabin. It was Simon Coddington, Silver Wig. The ship was searched end to end. He was not on board.

'You think he's skedaddled with the Carmichael girl?' Kevin asked me. We both had our elbows on the rail of the crew deck, staring out over the blue ocean.

'Yeah,' I said, 'unless he's water-skiing on a very long rope.'

Chapter Three

One minute the sunshine life, a randy actress waiting in Cabin 71 . . .

The next I was watching rain skidding down the carriage windows as the boat train rattled through Wimbledon. Dawn was coming up over the grime of Wandsworth. The old bums were still snoring on the benches of Waterloo Station.

It felt great to be back.

I'm not joking as it happens. London can be a right drag in many ways but whenever I'm anywhere else I get this nagging feeling inside of me that real life is going on without me back there in the smoke.

They do say that cockneys don't travel well.

Why should we? We're already there.

It was only a fifteen minute cab ride to my so-called temporary flat in Ravenscourt Park. Hammersmith looked pretty grim in the rain.

The flat was cold and stale. The radio news was full of stuff about new strikes, fuel crises, rocketing prices and general doom. I'd forgotten to bring back a new tin of shaving soap and the old one was down to a weak splutter. I could feel the blade attacking my lovely tan.

Penicillin was growing on the lonely pork pie in the fridge.

Then the car wouldn't start. The radio light had gone bust and that was probably why I hadn't noticed the radio was still on when I'd locked her up eighteen days before. I went back into the house to phone.

The garage promised to be round in five minutes and made it in an hour.

Because of a commuter rail strike the traffic was jammed

tight from Hammersmith Broadway to Kensington High Street. I shivered every yard of it because the heater had taken advantage of my absence to go on the blink.

I still wouldn't live anywhere else, if you can call it living.

'So you just sat tight?' Dot snapped.

'Well, a ship's a handy thing to have under you in the middle of the ocean, isn't it? What else should I have done?'

'They were the ones you were after – once they'd done a bunk you should've flown back from Malta.'

'There was no actual proof she was bent.'

'Really? She pays out near on five hundred to some punter on three hands of pontoon – then he jumps ship with her at Gibraltar? How much more bloody proof would you need? How the hell did they get tipped off you were on to them anyway?'

I could have made a guess but what difference?

'Christ! You know her references turned out to be fakes – *and* there's no such person as Simon Coddington at the address he gave?'

'Okay – so she was bent and he was her partner. That's solved the mystery, hasn't it?'

'Has it hell! Barclay and Marley made it quite clear – the main thing was to find out the system they were using.'

'She dealt him winning cards, that was all the system they needed.'

'That's all? This man faked a passport and bought a cruise ticket at eight hundred quid? Doesn't that sound like a fairly big caper to you?'

It was the first time Dot had given me a real coating. I could have told her that Kevin Barclay probably warned them accidentally. It would have sounded like an excuse.

'Okay,' I said snappily, 'let's say she's the bent one. He's a randy old sod with plenty of loot, he's on that boat to feel everything but seasick. He tries to pull her and she says Hullo Sailor, how about letting me deal you winning hands and we'll split the bunce? She could do that every trip with a different passenger.'

'Why jump ship then?'

'How the fuck would I know?'

We stared at each other. She'd been a good friend to me when my police career collapsed but one good turn doesn't deserve flesh and blood.

'You boobed and you've cost me money,' she said.

'Payment by results?' I sneered.

'Not payment by results! There was an additional fee for catching anybody weeding out the casino take.'

'How much?'

'None of your bloody business. What I can't take is you making me look a fool. You were quick enough to suss out that this Carmichael woman was bent and then you let her know you were on to her. I thought you were more professional than that.'

I stared at her. Maybe if I was a clever thinker I wouldn't be in this racket. A lot of the time I just do things and wonder why afterwards.

Maybe I'd been looking for an excuse.

Anyway I got to my feet and told her to stuff her job up her jumper and walked out.

I got into the mews and buttoned up my suede coat and got into the car and lit one of my duty-frees. What the hell did I do now? It was the coldest I'd felt since the lodger stole the blankets. I cannot tell a lie, I came near to losing my bottle.

I had about two hundred quid in the bank. I'd tried to set up on my own once before without enough capital and I knew how dodgy it was.

Bottle and glass – arse. It's rhyming. It depends how you pronounce glawss. It means shitting yourself.

Of course I had alternatives, like applying to be a council bailiff and helping to chuck homeless families into the street, or joining a big security outfit and getting a helmet and a big stick.

Then I told myself to get a grip. I drove out of the mews and turned right for the West End.

The estate agent's office was in Mortimer Street, in the rag trade area north of Oxford Street. I was attended to by a teenager who was only picking up the basics before turning himself into a property millionaire. You could tell he was a big thinker. First off he told me about a nifty opportunity in High Holborn, 95,000 square feet at £125,000 a year plus rates.

I bet he owned his first empty skyscraper before he was twenty-one.

'That one might suit me better when I hire fifteen thousand assistants,' I said wearily. 'Look, squire, I do debt-collecting and that, all I need's a room and a desk and somewhere for the Dobermanns to lie down between raids.'

'Oh, I see,' he said, dropping the 'sir'. Teenagers nowadays! 'Well we do have a double room in Mayfair, the last tenant was a private detective actually – a real one. He died recently. His wife has asked us to find somebody to take over the rest of the lease, it's got about two years to run. The rent is two hundred and thirty pounds per quarter – payable in advance, of course. The rates are about three pounds a week.'

I tried not to look like the man who couldn't get to sleep counting sheep because he couldn't see his fingers in the dark. It seemed to add up to more than twenty quid a week. I'd been hoping for nearer ten.

'You won't find anything cheaper in the West End,' said the telepathic little bastard.

I said I'd have a look at it. The quarter's rent in advance would clean out my bank account but he did say a double room and there might be a way of sub-letting the other office, I thought, being fairly quick in most ways except the important ones.

It was in Shepherd Market, that quaint little part between Curzon Street and Piccadilly, the sort of phoney London they put in Hollywood films, villagey, narrow streets and alleys, little brick buildings, tea-rooms, bull's-eye windows.

By night it changes.

When I was a bogey I was once called to a midnight disturbance in that quaint little village.

One of the mob of horny punters who pound through the little alleys looking for instant relief had decided to smash up this whore's gaff after being told he was too Brahms for a short time. Brahms and Lizst, pissed, if you get my meaning. The Shepherd Market brasses are a bit choosier than their Soho sisters, who turn away trade only if the customer is too legless to carry five quid up the stairs.

After we'd taken care of this nutter the brass told us she was paying seventy-five quid a week rent for her two rooms – the waiting-room had *Punch* on the coffee table – but she was still coining enough to send her son to a well-known snob school, Harrow or Winchester, I can't remember which.

She could have passed for forty-five on a dark night with a following wind. She said she preferred the bondage trade because most of them were toffs and gave no bother that a good whipping couldn't cure.

Who actually owned the building she didn't know. They don't boast about it, the respectable property kings who make the profits out of the Shepherd Market whores.

Number 147 Shepherd Market was an ordinary house door between a cake-shop and an empty window with a To Let notice. Jack the Lad in the estate agents had given me a string with three keys. The Chubb key opened the street door. I went up these narrow, squeaky stairs.

On the first floor landing there were two doors, one unmarked, the other with a sign, *Christine Bunn Secretarial Ltd.*

I went on up. The top landing had two doors. One was marked *Private*. The other had two panes of frosted glass and still carried the sign, *Fitch Private Investigations*. The lettering was ancient. Fitch must have set up shop when gents twirled waxy moustaches and worried duchesses hired discreet snoopers to trace the Hon Felicity's bastard son, now heir to the de Courcy Braithwaite estates.

I let myself in with a mortice key. The top floor was divided into two rooms. The rear one had a window that looked out at brick walls and other windows. It was empty. They hadn't taken away the faded red carpet, however, and bright patches showed where Fitch's furniture had been.

Opening the partition door I was in a much brighter front room that looked down on the sun-awnings of the shops in the little pedestrian alley.

I lit another duty-free and looked round the bare room.

When I was a kid in the East End we only read about places like Mayfair. Same city, sure enough, but as much to do with us as the moon.

At least we could look up and see the bleeding moon.

I knew plenty of people who'd only maybe been Up West to Piccadilly once in their whole lives. The movies made us better acquainted with New York and Chicago than we were with Mayfair.

From the window it didn't look too classy. Maybe I'd arrived thirty years too late.

If I did them a cheque for a quarter's rent I would have nothing left. How could I furnish the place? How would I eat for the first month or two, until I started earning?

A bell rang in the front room.

'Yeah well, there you go,' I said, taking a last look at where my classy black leather executive suite would have gone.

I looked up and crunched down the squeaky stairs.

When I opened the street door there was this middle-aged woman on the pavement. She was craning her neck to get her ear near the speaking grille. Her pale, narrow face didn't show a lot of enthusiasm for the looks of me. She tried to push past into the little lobby.

'Were you ringing the top floor, luv?' I said.

'Isn't Mr Fitch in?' she demanded, as if I was to blame for something.

'He's out in a case,' I said.

She thought I said on a case. Nobody listens these days.

'There must be somebody in his office,' she muttered, still trying to get past. I kept my hand on the door. She glared up at me. I held out the string with the three keys.

'Mr Fitch is dead, his office is empty,' I said.

'Oh.'

She put her hand to her face and nipped at the fingertips of her brown glove.

She had a slight twitch to the left side of her mouth. It always made me think she was going to smile. Between twitches she looked nearer to weeping.

'Are you – er – connected with Mr Fitch?' she asked, sounding a lot less stroppy.

'I was looking over his office.'

'Are you taking over his business?'

I cannot tell a lie, I told a lie.

'It's been offered to me,' I said, 'I'm in the same line of work if you've got a problem.'

And that was how I got my first client. As I say, at times I can move quite fast, even if I am going over cliffs.

Her name was Mrs Spencer.

'A friend recommended Mr Fitch to me,' she said, 'he helped with her divorce. He really is dead, is he?'

'If he wasn't before he must be by now – sorry, go on.'

Mrs Spencer put three spoons of white sugar into her tea and stirred it to death. She'd have been more at home in a cake-shop but the sight of fat matrons ramming the chocolate cakes in always gives me the urge to start a grapefruit diet.

'My husband was killed last week in the Underground at Tottenham Court Road,' she said at last. 'He fell under a train, you probably read about it.'

'No, I was out of the country.'

'They opened the inquest on Friday. It was adjourned but I know what they're going to say.'

'Suicide?'

'He would *never* have killed himself. Arthur was a *devout* man. He was having his troubles but he would never have brought such a stigma on himself. Or on me. He was the most considerate man on earth.'

'What happened?'

'That's just it. It looks like suicide. Three people said they

27

saw him pushing through the crowds to the very edge of the platform. But there was another woman – she told the station staff she saw him having an argument with some men, then she refused to give evidence. The police say there's nothing they can do about it. She says it wasn't Arthur she saw. Here's what the newspapers printed.'

She gave me two cuttings. It wasn't anything out of the ordinary. He'd been 53, suffering from a depression following redundancy after eighteen years as sales manager for a technical publishing firm that had been taken over. He'd gone that day to ask the new management for a job, any kind of job for at his age he couldn't get another executive number.

Under the rules of their staff pension scheme he was too old even to be taken on as a sales rep. He'd made a bit of a scene.

Afterwards he must have had a few drinks. Around the five o'clock rush hour at Tottenham Court Road tube station he'd shoved through the crowd in a hurry and fell on to the rails in front of an eastbound Central Line train. It had taken half an hour to free his body. The autopsy showed he'd consumed the equivalent of six large whiskies.

'It doesn't mention the other witness,' I said.

'I know. But she gave her name and address to the platform attendant at the time. When the police saw her she said she must've been mistaken – they showed her Arthur's photograph –'

'So what did you want Fitch to do?'

'See her, of course.'

'Get her to change her mind – again?'

'People are so callous these days, they don't want to become involved. In the war it was different – but they don't care any more. I thought if she knew what it meant to me –'

'Like appeal to her better nature?'

'Mr Hazell, I can honestly swear to God that Arthur would never have killed himself. I *knew* him, Mr Hazell, he would never have left me to face a stigma like that. We were both prominent in our local church, you know.'

'Okay, suppose this woman did see an argument. Where does

that get you? A description of some men in a tube station in the rush-hour? How many millions would the description fit?'

'That's what everybody keeps telling me. But couldn't they put the description on that television programme, Police Five? Maybe they'd come forward if they knew how important it was. It's a chance, isn't it? What else can I do? I could never enjoy another moment's peace in my whole life if I thought I hadn't done everything possible to . . .'

She touched at her nose with her gloved hand.

I lit another duty-free and looked at her funny velvet chapeau and the two moles on her knobbly chin.

'You see, Arthur and I were alone,' she said looking down at her tea. 'We had a son but he was drowned at Bognor when he was eleven. Arthur always used to say he hoped I'd go first – it sounds cruel but he meant that one of us would be going through a lot of loneliness when the other died and he wanted to spare me that. I *know* he would never have taken his own life.'

I stubbed out the Rothmans. I never like the brands they sell on ships or aeroplanes. I always buy a carton because they're cheap but I always stub them out quick.

'You got the address for this other woman?' I said.

She gave me a sheet of blue writing paper torn from a pad. Mrs Phyllis Locke, 24, Laburnum Court, Maida Vale.

'If you want I'll go and have a word with her,' I said.

'That's very kind of you – but, well, I was going to ask Mr Fitch what it would cost before I –'

'Not more than ten pounds – just to have a word with her.'

'Oh.' Her face lit up. She reached for her handbag.

'No, pay me after,' I said. 'Give me your number and address, I'll get back to you when I've seen her.'

'It's all right, Mister Hazell, I'm old enough to know an honest face when I see one.'

'I shouldn't go too much on faces, Mrs Spencer, half the hooks in London look like bleeding cherubs.'

But in the street she suddenly shoved out a gloved hand and pressed a little roll of oncers into my greasy palm.

'I'm not actually poor, you know,' she said, with a brave smile, 'I really do appreciate your help.'

I cannot tell a lie, I was embarrassed. Only a tenner but it made me feel I was robbing the poor widow's larder.

As I say, I'm like the weather forecast, only bright in patches.

Chapter Four

I've never thought of Maida Vale as being anywhere in particular, just a place you go through to get to Irish Kilburn. It's all flats in Maida Vale, flats and rooms and people who come from somewhere else. Occasionally people get murdered there. More often than not the neighbours don't know their names.

I found the block of flats known as Laburnum Court after asking directions of no more than four people; three of them looked like our own but had worse English than me. The fourth was a Nigerian who had better English than me.

It was off Sutherland Avenue. It wasn't a posh block but it did have locked glass doors and a speaking grille system. I pressed number 24. The grille said nothing.

I rang the bell marked *Porter* a few times but that didn't win any jackpots. I rang number 23.

'I'm trying to find Mrs Locke rather urgently,' I said when a man's voice floated out of the box.

'You'd better come up,' he said.

On the buzz I pushed through the glass doors and took a shaky lift to the second floor.

He was waiting for me at the door of his flat. He must have approved of me, from the gorgeous smile I got. He was around fifty going on his second face-lift. From behind him came a heady mixture of soft music and sweet perfume.

'Did you say you were looking for Phyllis or George?' he said.

'Phyllis actually. Is she –'

'I say, do you like Chinese tea? I've just put a brew in motion. Would you like to come in and wait?'

Maybe it was the blue-rinse that made me hesitate.

'How long is she likely to be?'

'What day is it? Monday? Honest – I can never keep track. No, on Mondays she's usually home quite early. But do come in –'

'It's urgent. Is she at work?'

'Is it about the gas conversion? Because you'll be wanting to check my appliances anyway and –'

'No, it's personal. What time does she usually get home?'

'Monday? About half-past six usually. *Please* don't think you'll be putting me out, it's so nice to have someone to chat to.'

Only four hours to kill – over a cup of Chinese tea? He must have been desperate for a bit of company or a bit of something.

'Thanks but it is urgent,' I said.

He was disappointed but he told me she was the cutting-room manageress in a dress shop in Oxford Street, not too far from Bourne and Hollingsworth. He watched me go back along the corridor. As I waited for the lift I gave him a smile.

He waved and shut his door.

I drove back down Edgware Road and along Oxford Street and took less than twenty minutes to get parked.

The downstairs fitting-room of the ladies' dress-shop was air-conditioned but you don't get rid of the fragrance of a million women that easily. I coughed. A girl came out from behind a purple screen. I asked for Mrs Locke. She went back behind the screen.

Out came this jolly lady with a Cleopatra hairdo and a plump, cheeky face. She wasn't far short of forty, older than I normally go for but tasty. Her two-piece suit was a light-green that brought out her dark colouring and tanned skin. Her hair was jet black and her eyes were all of a twinkle under false eye-lashes big enough to keep the rain off her feet.

'Yes?' she said, all smile.

'Mrs Phyllis Locke I presume?'

'Do you really?' Her eyes never left mine, not from that first moment. 'That's me.'

'My name's James Hazell,' I said, 'I wonder if I could have a word with you.'

'Sounds intriguing, will it cost me money?'

'You have my word on it – no. It's personal.'

'Men with fair hair and blue eyes aren't to be trusted, my mother always told me.'

'She the one you got your looks from?'

'Oh!' She smiled saucily. 'You're awful – but I like you.'

I heard somebody coming down the stairs.

'You want to serve the customer and I'll wait?' I was trying to give myself a few moments to work out the right approach. She seemed jolly enough, a real goer in fact, but the law hadn't made any impression on her. She called the girl to attend the two women customers and then came back to me.

By this time our eyes were having a different conversation altogether.

'It's not going to cost you and it's not about natural gas conversion,' I said. Her eyebrows lifted. 'I was speaking to your neighbour in Number twenty-three –'

'What – Eunice? It all sounds very mysterious. You aren't police, are you?'

'No. Listen, could we have a chat when you pack up work? It won't take long but it is rather delicate. We could have a drink somewhere.'

'I can hardly wait.'

I took the keys back to the estate agents in Mortimer Street and told young Mr Big I'd think about the Shepherd Market office. He said that would probably be too late as people were trampling each other in the stampede to rent it.

I then went to the Post Office in Soho Street and phoned a couple of geezers who ran small agencies – divorce work, bad debts, that sort of thing. They both said keep in touch, Jim old mate, but business is very slack right now.

A brilliant future stretched ahead of me, snatchback jobs for car firms, hounding pensioners who'd got behind with the telly payments, credit checking for shylocks calling themselves finance houses, window-peeping at husbands and wives who thought this time it was all going to be heaven.

I was outside on the pavement when Phyllis Locke appeared. She was wearing a crocodile-skin coat. It was ten to six. The pavement was thick with people who had somewhere worth hurrying to.

'Where do you fancy for a drink?' I said.

'You're the man, you make the decisions.'

We walked to the car in Marlborough Street. As she was getting in her coat crackled against the seat. She was all shine and colour. She caught me looking at her and immediately pushed her chin up and smoothed back the skin on her throat.

'Don't tell me, double chin,' she said.

'And both as lovely as the other,' I said in a jolly voice.

'You're awful but I like you.' It was something they were all saying that year, a TV comedian's catchphrase.

I drove along to Marble Arch and then down Bayswater Road to White's Hotel. I've always fancied those big white hotels that face on to Hyde Park. The Mediterranean touch, I suppose, balconies with blue sun-awnings – the little things that mean class to your average herbert.

There was nobody else in the groundfloor cocktail bar. She asked for a small whisky. I had a bottle of tonic with ice and lemon.

'Don't you drink?' she asked, opening her crackly coat.

'Only when I'm depressed.'

'You don't look the depressed type to me.'

'That's why I never drink.'

We looked at each other across the table. Sometimes you can be too clever so I gave it to her straight.

'I'm an enquiry agent,' I said, 'that woman whose husband fell under the tube train is paying me to find out if you'll change your mind about giving evidence. It means a lot to her not to have it down to suicide.'

She touched the little Spanish curl at her ear. Her lips rolled over each other.

'All my blind dates go wrong,' she said. She pinched the tanned skin above her adam's apple. 'I'm sorry, I made a mistake, it wasn't the same man.'

'Well that's okay then,' I said, sitting back and looking relieved. 'She paid me to ask you and now I've asked you, haven't I? I told her it was a waste of time and money but some people won't be told, will they?'

I smiled at her. She scratched the back of her hand with her plum-coloured nails. She picked up her glass and took a sip and then moved it in little circles, watching the whisky swirl.

She rubbed the skin under her chin. Then she looked me straight in the eye. I got in first.

'All she paid me was a lousy ten quid,' I said, 'you doing anything special or would you like to help me spend it?'

'You know that feeling when little bells ring in your head?' she said softly. 'Right from the first moment?'

'Me, too,' I said.

'My husband's in Brighton on a motivation course. We can go back to my flat if you like.'

'Yeah, lovely.'

Because of the old queen she called Eunice we went in separately. I dropped her off up the street and parked the Stag. I waited five minutes to let her give Eunice the elbow. Seemingly he spent his lonely evenings planning excuses to drop in for a chat.

Then I went up to the front entrance of Laburnum Court and pushed the bell, just once and lightly.

The door lock buzzed. I went up the stairs so that Eunice wouldn't hear the lift.

'Sure you won't have a drink?' she said when we were in the living-room. She called it the lounge. It wasn't all that big but it was holding a lot of expensive gear. Lots of fancy sidelights, a waterbed divan, hi-fi speakers, a remote control handset for the colour TV, modern armchairs that looked like hollowed-out eggs, glossy book club editions of the great unread masters, abstract paintings to match the walls, white Indian rugs on parquet flooring, a glass coffee-table inlaid with pictures of vintage sports cars, and not a mark on any of it.

Not a stain, not a scratch, not a spot. Not a thing out of place. Everything as new as the shop window.

And as dead.

I didn't have to ask if they had any kids.

'It's silly but I'm nervous,' she said, patting at her shiny black hair with her plump brown hands. 'I haven't actually done this before – not here.'

'Me neither – not here.'

'Do you want to go to the bathroom?'

'Why not?'

'I'll be in here.' She walked to the door that led into the bedroom.

'Okay, if I'm longer than two minutes start without me.'

'You're awful but I like you,' she said. It was just something she said out of habit, mechanical almost, not far short of being bloody irritating.

When I came into the bedroom she was already between the sheets. They had two single beds. The only light came from the door to the lounge. Far off I heard an ambulance siren. I stood above her, hauling up my black polo neck sweater. She just lay there.

'Not much light in here,' I said, kicking off my leather casuals. 'I really need to see your knees to get me going.'

'My knees?' she giggled nervously. 'I've never heard of anyone being kinky about knees before.'

'Nothing kinky about it,' I said. I climbed in beside her. 'Where's the switch for this thing?' I asked, leaning across her to the bedside lamp on the white table between the beds. Her body stiffened. She was still wearing something.

'We don't need the light,' she said, one hand holding the sheet to her chin, the other pulling my arm down.

'You said it – the man makes the decisions,' I said. My fingers found the switch. She stared up at me, her black eyelashes blinking rapidly. 'What's the matter – knees trembling, are they?'

She turned her face away. I kissed the back of her neck and her solid brown shoulders. I felt for her breasts but she had her arms clutched across her chest. I lifted them clear. She turned quickly towards me and pulled herself close. I pushed the blankets off. She was still wearing a black nylon slip.

I got my hands under it and bent down and kissed her warm brown stomach. Then I worked my way up. The reason for all this nervousness was staring me in the face. She had no nipples.

She waited for me to say something.

'You got no raspberry ripples,' I said cheerily, 'you only got little dents.' I kissed both dents. 'Cor – this could cure a man of knees.'

'Men like nipples,' she said, as if accusing me of something.

'I've been weaned as it happens.'

I kissed her on the mouth, at the same time working the slip up to her shoulders and pulling it over her arms. Her body was solid, no bones sticking out, nice fat thighs, white where her bikini had been. She had big breasts that were quite firm.

'I want to kiss you all over,' I said. I started to prove it but she grabbed hold of my head.

'No – do it properly,' she murmured impatiently.

'Just let me –'

'No! I want to feel you inside me, all of you, *please*, I want you so much.'

She gripped me with her arms and knees and mouth and I got a grip on her and the game, as your sports page Hemingways say, came to life. We rolled over and she squirmed on top of me, her breasts on my chest, her black hair falling on to my face, both of us panting and rubbing and moaning wonderful wonderful.

'Wasn't it good for you, too?' she murmured when we were resting in each other's arms afterwards.

'Yeah – terrific.'

'But you didn't –'

'Don't worry about it.'

'Yes, but I'd like to make it good for you as well.'

So I told her about a woman called Toni Abrey who'd spat in my face.

'I didn't know I was in love with her till that moment,' I said. 'It was a custody case and she thought I'd been helping the other woman to steal her little girl. It looked as though I'd only been rumping her as part of the job I expect. When she spat in my face – well, it just seemed to freeze me inside. I suppose it sounds silly but quite often I can actually still feel her spit on my cheek and my eye and I go to rub it off. Silly, I suppose.'

'It doesn't sound silly to me,' she said stroking my head. 'I know how it can happen. My husband went queer on me. You met Eunice – we'd been going to some of his parties and next thing – I don't blame my husband, I suppose it was there all the time. He's gone through hell with it. We still love each other but he can't bear me even touching him. He's scared to death his firm will find out.'

'It's legal now.'

'Not actually popular though, is it, not with that kind of employer. It wouldn't be so bad if he went gay completely but he's not like that. He goes to a psychiatrist every week. He hates it but he can't help it.'

'Frightened of publicity, is he?'

'They can get involved with some very slimy specimens. A lot of them go in for blackmail – even if it's legal it isn't something you want people to know about. Especially in George's kind of job.'

'That's why you couldn't risk getting involved in Mrs Spencer's case, wasn't it?'

'I'm sorry for her but her husband is dead – mine's still got a chance.'

Our noses were almost touching. Her eyes had to move from side to side to look into mine.

'I can't see what you had to worry about,' I said, brushing the hair off her forehead.

'It was George who was worried.' She pulled her face back to get a good look at me. 'I don't even care if you're only doing this to get me talking. It doesn't matter anyway – they can't make me give evidence.'

'That's true.'

I kissed her eyes.

'It *was* that man Spencer I saw. You know those horrible men who diddle people out of their money playing cards in the street?'

'The three-card trick mob?'

'That's who he was having the argument with. You know that part in Tottenham Court Road tube where there's a mirror in the corner? I heard them shouting before I got to the corner. One of them gave him a push. He sat down on the stairs and they ran for it. He dropped his bowler hat. He must have hurt his spine, he was in agony when he tried to get up. I picked up his bowler hat for him before anybody could tramp on it. He ran down the stairs after them. I didn't see him falling off the platform, it was very crowded and I was going on the other platform for Oxford Circus. Then I heard all this fuss and the people started pushing back through those connecting bits – they were clearing the other platform. Somebody said a man with a bowler hat had fallen under the train. I said I'd seen him having a row – I didn't know it was the same man, I just seemed to assume it was – anyway, the platform attendant heard me and asked for my name and address. I wasn't really thinking – but when I got home George went potty. It wouldn't have been so bad if it had been an ordinary accident but he said with criminals involved I might have to identify them and then I'd be the only witness that they'd been having an argument. Criminals like that always try to interfere with witnesses – George was hysterical. He said they'd come here and try to bribe us – or maybe terrorize us. He said they might find out about him being queer and use that. I said he was just being hysterical but he made me swear I wouldn't tell the police anything. He's pathological about the slightest chance of people finding out.'

'Yeah. He's not a bad judge as it happens. These chaps are not slow to find a weakness. How did you know they were boardsmen – three-card trick merchants?'

'I see them often enough in Oxford Street. That lot in particular. There were two of them – a big blond one with a horrible face and a little bald one. He's the one who deals the cards whenever I see them – he's got a real cheeky face – you'd think if you met him anywhere else he'd be a lot of fun to know – then you see him swindling people out of their money.

In the shop we're always talking about why the police can't put an end to it.'

'What did you mean about the other one's horrible face?'

'He's got pock-marks – all over his cheeks. Oooh, he's repulsive.' She shuddered.

'So you think Spencer was chasing them?'

'It looked like it.'

'Funny. Three witnesses said he fell – nobody pushed him. Unless – of course, that's it! He was chasing them and the only way he could get up the platform was at the very edge, people always leave about a foot clear there in case the train hits them. He was chasing up the edge and he lost his balance, it would've looked like he jumped deliberately. So my widow was right after all!'

Chapter Five

'I wish I could help her but I'm not giving evidence, you do know that?'

'Yeah.'

'Even if you tell the police what I've just told you now I'll deny it. I gave my solemn oath to George. Nobody will make me change my mind.'

Her hand stopped rubbing up and down my back. Our eyes were so close we could see our own reflections. Then her knee began to push between my thighs.

'Are you only doing this to get me talking?' she said, looking at me sadly.

'Oh yeah, I'm a real shit. Think I'd last long in my racket if I wasn't? This is how I get all my information. Comes a bit hard with lorry-drivers, though.'

'Oh my God,' she said, closing her eyes and throwing back her head, 'every time you do that I feel like a nymphomaniac.'

I woke up about two in the morning and got out of bed. She opened her eyes and saw me pulling on my strides.

'Stay till morning if you like,' she said, 'I could make you breakfast – George won't be back till Thursday.'

I sat on the bed, pulling my socks.

'No, I'll push off now,' I said.

'I wish I had you in my bed every night.'

I pulled down the blankets and leaned over and kissed her gently on the buttocks. Then I covered her with the blankets and kissed her on the mouth.

'Even if you were only trying to trick me I can still hear little bells,' she said softly.

She got up and put on a brushed nylon nightie. She came

with me to the door. Without the false eyelashes and in her bare feet she looked a lot younger and a lot less confident. She put her finger to her lips and pointed up the corridor at Eunice's door.

'Was it worth it?' she whispered in my ear.

'But of course – I got what I came for, didn't I?'

She smiled up at me. 'I like you but you're awful,' she said.

'I'll ring you,' I murmured.

She shook her head.

'No you won't,' she whispered, her eyes on mine, 'they never do.'

I drove down Edgware Road, then Westway to Wood Lane and Shepherd's Bush Green, then Goldhawk Road to Ravenscourt Park. Even at three in the morning the traffic was bombing along, all of us night travellers getting back to our own beds, the drunk, the desperate and the disappointed. *They never do?*

I despise self-pity, specially in other people.

I woke up about eight. I got into the bath and switched on the transistor. The news on all channels was the usual doom so I put on the non-stop pop and cogitated till the water got too cold.

I started to shave and then remembered I still needed a can of soap. The face in the mirror didn't look as if it was just back from a Mediterranean cruise.

I put on the other pair of socks and then opened a can of baked beans and ate them cold with a teaspoon. I had a cup of tea without milk. I prefer it with milk but there wasn't any. Jackie would have hated me living like this. Funny, wasn't it, she left me for this other berk because I was on the booze something rotten and now I'd beaten the bottle, only it was too late because they were married and living in Chigwell with a baby.

What a dope I'd been.

I felt bloody terrible. I'd been six months in that flat and apart from a few paperbacks and my clothes there was nothing in it that belonged to me.

So what could I do? Buy an electric blanket and pretend it was a cosy little home? Sod that. Jackie leaving me like that had put me off the cosy home-life for good. I was well organized, wasn't I? I ate in cafes and took the filthiest stuff to the launderette and sometimes even remembered to clean the bath.

Oh yeah, great.

Where the hell was Miss Right?

I phoned Mrs Spencer, out there in swinging Ruislip. I'd only been there once. I was pissed and fell asleep in the Central Line tube and woke up at the end of the line. Never saw a lot of Ruislip to have much opinion of it, really.

On the phone her voice sounded a lot jollier. Maybe her face was necessary for the full sadness effect.

'Mrs Locke told me what she saw,' I said, 'but there's no way she'll change her mind about giving evidence, I'm afraid. Your husband was most likely having a ruck with a team of street con-men – you know what the three-card trick is? From the sound of it he was chasing them and fell off the platform accidentally.'

'I knew it was something like that! I knew it! That means we can tell the police and –'

'She'll deny even speaking to me.'

'But the police –'

'They didn't make much headway with her before, did they?'

'Well we can't just leave it like that.'

'Even if the law did collar these blokes they aren't going to own up to anything. Villains like them have been admitting nothing to the law since they could talk.'

'What can I do then?'

'I really don't know, Mrs Spencer.'

'I'm certainly not going to sit back and do nothing. Couldn't you try to speak to these men, Mr Hazell? They might tell you things they wouldn't tell the police.'

'It's possible – if I could get hold of them. They're the slipperiest villains in London. The law doesn't seem to be able to nab 'em working the three-card caper in Oxford Street in broad daylight. They dodge about, ten minutes here, off to another pitch – one sniff of bother and they're off quicker than a bride's nightie.'

'But you could *try* to find them, couldn't you? I don't mind paying you another ten pounds, Mr Hazell.'

I put my palm over the mouthpiece and blew a sigh.

'Mrs Spencer, you don't get a proper enquiry agent for less than twenty-five quid a day. That ten quid was just petrol money. I'd like to help but –'

'I really don't know much about these things –'

'Look, even if you're J. Paul Getty and hire the FBI – what happens when you track them down? You think a three-card trick mob will bowl along to a coroner's court to admit that one of their victims got killed because they skinned him?'

'It means an awful lot to me, Mr Hazell.'

'I know but –'

'I do have some money, Mr Hazell. I'll spend every penny of it to stop them blackening Arthur's name. If you got them to tell you what happened – couldn't you give the evidence yourself at the inquest? My solicitor told me most coroners try not to bring in a verdict of suicide. They'd listen to you, wouldn't they?'

'Possible. The rules aren't so strict in a coroner's court. But it's all very iffey, Mrs Spencer, finding them is –'

'I'm sure you're very clever at that sort of thing, Mr Hazell. Couldn't we at least meet and talk it over?'

So that was how I kicked in my steady wages and got my first client and started to shoe it up and down Oxford Street on a cold, damp day in February. I didn't really go a bundle on Mrs Spencer's cut-rate but I had a solid hundred quid.

I thought about it for an hour or so. Two hundred and thirty quid a quarter was nine hundred and twenty a year, twenty quid a week. Plus rates, electric, phone? Freedom is more pricey than fish these days.

Then I thought – what the hell and went to my bank in Shaftesbury Avenue. I paid in her cheque and they got me a print-out of my account. With her donation I had three hundred and twenty-seven quid. It wasn't really enough but the way inflation was going it was shrinking every minute so I took a taxi to the estate agents in Mortimer Street.

The Shepherd Market office was still on the market. I signed them a cheque and gave my bank and Dot Wilmington as references. She was a good sort, Dot, she wouldn't hold our row against me.

They gave me the keys and said the lease could be signed when they'd checked my references. I used their phone to make appointments with the Post Office telephones and the Electricity Board. Wheels were in motion. I walked back to Oxford Street.

Against a blank bit of wall between a gents' outfitters and a souvenir tourist trap I saw two empty cardboard boxes. I couldn't remember seeing them before. Just rubbish? Or put one on top and what did you have? A gaming table on the quick.

That's all the equipment the three-card mob need to make a living. Plus a bundle of fivers for luring money – and three cards, of course.

Maybe they were about!

I walked on to Soho Square and fed my meter. No sooner were the coins in than it started to rain. Heavy stuff, no weather for three-carders. I resented leaving all that free time to some other bastard but there was no point in hanging about . . .

I phoned cousin Tel about furniture that night from Ravenscourt Park.

'Hullo, Jim-Jim,' he said, 'how's my hero keepin' in the great big town? Plenty ov everythin', eh?'

'Oh everything's quite jolly. How's Sheree and the kids?'

'Top ov the bill all round. So wot're you after then?'

'Much furniture falling off lorries these days?'

'Wot sort ov furniture?'

'Office gear. It has to be kosher stuff mind, I'm in Mayfair now you know.'

'Mayfair? Straight up? How's that then?'

'I kicked that job into touch. I got my first client already but it's a bit strong asking people to sit on a bare floor.'

'Hang about, Jim-Jim, them saucepans are kickin' up hell here.'

I could hear the kids screaming in the background. My flat seemed very quiet. His Sheree has cousin Tel well under the cosh but he thrives on it. I supposed he was a good father but never having had any saucepan lids of my own I could have been a bad judge.

'As it happens I'm seein' my friend Slippery tomorrer,' said Tel, 'I'll have a word wiv him. Wot you thinkin' about – desk an' chairs an' that?'

'Use your initiative – just remember it's for Mayfair.'

'Much you intendin' to splash out on all this gear?'

'Thirties?'

'How the bleedin' hell you expeckta furnish an office for thirty fakkin nicker?'

'If I had the bread I'd be going to a proper furniture shop, wouldn't I? By the way, tell you what I would like, a small fridge, if that's possible.'

'A desk, coupla chairs, few bits an' pieces an' a small fridge – all for thirty quid? You don't want me back teeth as well for a nicker do yer?'

'No, only if you're giving them away.'

'Here, I've only seen yer Mum yesterday, haven't I? She's only asked me why you ain't bin around there for ages, hasn't she?'

'I was on a Mediterranean cruise, wasn't I?'

'Mayfair – Mediterranean cruises? All go for our Jim-Jim, innit? Cor. Lissen – why don't you come out Saturday night wiv Sheree an' me, up the Three Colts for a few, see some of the old chaps, bring a bird an' we'll have a Chinese after, yeah?'

'It would be nice, Tel, only this case is a round-the-clock job. Thanks for asking.'

'All right. Anyway, give us a bell tomorrer night.'

'Okay. Love to Sheree and the saucepans.'
'Cheers.'

Next morning, Thursday, the sky was blue and I knew I'd have to put in a whole day on the pavement. I also had meets with the phone engineer and the electric.

Still, I could always take things easy when I was dead, couldn't I?

Chapter Six

The big walk.

I'll tell you what makes Oxford Street so stony-hearted. There's no place to stop unless you're spending money and whatever way you're going the crowds are going the other.

A river of faces and me struggling against the tide both ways.

Still, there are compensations. Any London bloke will always tell you – wherever you go in the world you can't beat the birds in Oxford Street. Mind you, half of them are foreign.

It's like a show. There's the Hare Krishners jiving along to divine bliss. There's all sorts, like the geezer who parades about with the big placard – *Less Lust by Less Proteins*.

According to his sign another cause for all this modern randiness is Sitting.

Sitting?

To take my mind off my feet I went across and gave him a bob for his pamphlet – *Eight Passion Proteins*, a little yellow book he's had printed.

The eight passion proteins, he says, are meat, fish and bird; cheese, eggs; peas, beans and lentils – and Sitting.

Sitting?

Read on: 'Those who sit down to work and those who are inclined to idleness should remember that physical inactivity conserves proteins, so that they become available for passion.'

I wasn't going to have much available the way my legs felt.

The West End does attract 'em, no doubt about it. Nutters and mutterers and weirdos of all sizes. In the amusement hall they were shoulder to shoulder at the penny machines, suckers for the old sport of giving your money to somebody else and getting nothing back for it.

A girl six foot passed, teetering. Her hair was green at the front and orange at the back. She wasn't really that tall, just that her shoes had eight-inch soles.

An ambulance hooter made the heads turn.

It went round an island the wrong side. You hear an ambulance screaming roughly every ten minutes in Oxford Street. Maybe it's the same one doing laps. When Jackie was a nurse she said most of the ambulance crews put on the hooter to get home quicker or back to base for a crucial tea transfusion. I said everybody knew *that*. If all those sirens were for real there would have to be armies of casualties dropping like flies round every corner.

You never actually *see* anybody being lifted into an ambulance, do you?

I missed having silly little chats like that with Jackie.

Three days steady flogging it up and down Oxford Street was just what the doctor had not ordered for my wonky ankle but by Thursday I couldn't feel any pain. Maybe it had dropped off, I didn't like to look.

Three days steady pounding through crowds could drive anybody round the twist. Pedestrians should keep to the left like cars. The slower and older people are the more room they want to take up. They resent you for trying to walk faster. They'll even make up a line of backs to stop you.

Just a little bit mad. The never-ending crowds, all walking the wrong way, the pushing, the noise, the umbrellas looking for eyes, the fake party music blasting out of the boutiques, the cold wind whipping all the way up from Hyde Park, the bitter faces, the suspicious faces, the moronic faces – even the beautiful faces become too much in the end because that's what it is about Oxford Street – the people have no end to them.

You begin to think the doom merchants are right, the world is too crowded, in a minute we're going to starve to death standing on each other's toes.

So you take a grip and try to see the bright side. How about a Japanese woman wearing a white smog mask? Six French tourists who *weren't* shoving everybody else into the gutter?

Three Italians talking quietly!

I saw an American lose the battle for a cab. The British lion still has teeth.

Then comes Thursday late shopping night and you begin to yearn for desert islands. The shops stay open at night so the people come flocking in from morning on. It's the guvnor day for crowds, something like twenty-five thousand shoppers barging about the pavements, some geezer playing Scotch bagpipes, police with loud-hailers trying to control the mobs.

Mind you, I was only covering the bit between Oxford Circus and Tottenham Court Road.

God knows what it was like in the busy part.

As soon as the light began to go I did likewise. Three-carders don't like the dark. The dog-eyes might miss a copper.

It was ten past five when I got into Shepherd Market, only twenty minutes of meter rule to go. I took a chance and parked on a yellow line.

Going up the stairs to my new *Mayfair* office I met a pair of feet. Next I met her legs. She was wearing black tights but the shape seemed reasonable.

'Oh – are you the chap who's taking over from Mr Fitch?' she said, in the poshest of lah-di-dahs.

'Yeah. My name's James Hazell.'

The stairs were narrow and I wasn't carrying the etiquette book to see what it says about squeezing past a lady. I knew that blocking her passage wasn't the done thing. The light was behind her and I couldn't see her face too well, my eyes being level with her knees.

'I'm Christine Bunn,' she said. 'I run a little secretarial agency on the first floor. Are you moving in soon?'

'I'm in already, I'm waiting for furniture.'

'I've got a key for you,' she said, 'it's for the loo. That's this other door up here.' She turned and started back up the stairs. 'Mr Fitch and I always kept it locked. Would you like it now?'

'It could save embarrassment,' I said.

We reached the landing. She was about twenty-six or seven. She had light brown hair cut almost as short as men's hair used to be. Her skin was beautiful, no make-up, just inner radiance. She was on the petite side but elegant with it. She had a smallish face with a wide mouth and very white teeth. Not a little plastic dolly, either, her nose came out a fair bit and when she smiled there was just a touch of Mr Punch.

A little corker.

The only snag was that drippy accent.

When I speak to the likes of cousin Tel I can hear how my voice has lost the real gorblimeys but compared to her I was forty fousand fevvers on a frush.

Still, we were already on loo-sharing terms. Can't get a better ice-breaker than that, can you?

She unlocked her office door. I stood there while she dug out the carsi key from her desk.

'Why d'you bother to lock it anyway?' I asked.

'I have so many girls traipsing in and out all day and Mr Fitch used to have some extremely dubious visitors so we decided to keep it nice and clean for ourselves. Will you be having dubious visitors?'

'I expect so but I'll warn 'em to spend their pennies before they get here.'

She gave me a quick look.

'Any other arrangements I should know about?' I asked.

'I don't think so. Are you a private detective?'

'Enquiry agent doesn't sound so flash. You fancy a drink and I'll tell you about my best cases?'

'No,' she said, bluntly. 'I don't drink.'

'Cup of tea then?'

'Men are so boringly predictable,' she said, snootily, 'one gets so tired of –'

'I only said a cup of tea, darlin'.'

'One thing about Mr Fitch he was the old-fashioned gentleman type.' She was very good at sarcasm. She locked her door. 'To look at, you would have taken him for a schoolmaster or a vicar.'

'That must of bin thrillin' for yer, I'm always gittin' mistook for a hooligan an' that, in I?'

'Really?' she sniffed, snotty little bitch. She went down the stairs. Seemed like we'd got off to a bad start.

The hell with her.

After we'd got the stuff out of the van and up the stairs Tel wanted me to go with him and his oppo Rodney for a light ale, as he always described it. I said no.

Next thing he was coming up from the desk drawer with an automatic pistol pointing at me.

'Come on,' he snarled, pointing the black hole right at my guts, 'a light ale won't hurt yer. Think yer too high an' mighty to drink wiv us common herberts?'

'What the hell's that?' I said in a strangely high-pitched voice, one shaking finger pointing at the pistol. I knew he wouldn't have shot me deliberately but he was the reckless sort who drove without a licence and I could already hear him saying sorry for the gun accident at my funeral.

'It's a shooter, Jim,' he said quietly, 'any last requests?'

Although Tel is younger than me he is actually my uncle, which is why I call him cousin Tel, out of respect. He's a bit dodgy at times. A mad bastard you could say. I swallowed hard.

Then he threw it at me.

It was one of those plastic replica jobs, a Walther PPK auto. I caught it and let my shoulders drop with relief. I could see why people wanted them banned – unless you could feel how light it was you'd never know it for a toy.

'Banks have bin robbed wiv them things,' said his oppo Rodney.

I threw it back at cousin Tel.

'I bought it off this geezer to give to the kids,' he said, 'only Sheree won't have it in the house. Next thing they'll want a kosher job, she says, silly cow. You have it, Jim, give yer offis a bit ov class.'

He dropped it back into the drawer.

'You want this cheque made out to cash?' I said, kicking myself for having fallen for it.

'I'd sooner have readies but you wouldn't float a kite on me, would yer, Jim-Jim?' I started writing out the cheque. 'Me an' Rod's thought we'd git up the Wardorf Club for a quick one, haven't we, Rod? Not fancy it?'

'The Wardorf? They still got the rule about parking your bayonets at the door?'

'Go on! There's no bovver inside the club, is there Rod?'

'Only sometimes,' said Rod.

'I dunno how yer can live wivout a bit ovva drink now an' then.' Tel looked round the room. 'Yeah well, yer fixed up nice an' cosy now, ain't yer? If I hears ov anybody wantin' some sleuthin' done I'll put them on to yer. An' do try an' drop over yer Mum's place, wonchyer?'

'Yeah yeah.'

'Cheers.'

I sat behind the desk for ten minutes or so. It had seen a bit of service, a big solid job with three drawers on either side. For my money I'd also got a swivel chair, two small easy chairs, a little wooden table that Tel said would polish up a treat – and a small fridge.

Tel wouldn't have thanked me for asking too many questions but the fridge was a curious item. Wherever it had been before they'd been in a hurry to bring it away. Instead of unplugging it they'd cut the flex with scissors, leaving about six inches of wire hanging down the back.

Maybe it snapped when it fell off the lorry.

When I got outside there was a ticket under the wiper.

I screwed up the Cellophane envelope and tossed it over my shoulder on to the back seat with all the others. I'd worry about them when the government sent one of their cute reminders.

Driving home round Hammersmith Broadway I saw the bills for a fiendish horror movie and decided to see it. The reviews had been raves but it turned out to be a nonsense, tricky camera work in the alleys of Venice and a story a defending counsel wouldn't have swallowed. Still, it was a warm place to sit and eat cashew nuts.

That night in bed I had a brainwave. Why didn't I turn the back room of the office into a bedroom? That would save the rent of a flat.

The lease probably said the premises were banned for residential use but that was only words on paper.

As cousin Tel always says, rules is only for them with no bottle.

I had a lot of bad dreams that night and woke up feeling diabolical. I looked out of the window, groaning at the prospect of another lousy day on my pegs. It was a wet, miserable morning but it wasn't actually raining.

By ten o'clock I was doing my first lap of Soho Square. A minor bang on the bumper from a Mercedes, two arguments and roughly ten laps later I got a meter. It started to drizzle.

I shoved three shillings in the slot, giving me an hour and a half before feeding time. I pulled up the collar of my black raincoat and stuck both hands in my pockets.

Four or five bums were standing together under the overhanging roof of the genuine Tudor garden shed in the Square garden. As I got near I heard this hoarse Scotch voice.

'Ach, see this beggin' in the rain – s'no that good, is it?'

They all nodded, cigarette smoke climbing through the misty rain.

As I went round the shed a small bloke left the group and walked alongside me. I didn't stop. His hair was flat and his jacket was never going to get dry.

'I'm an alcoholic,' he announced, 'how about a few pence for my first drink?'

'You want me to *help* you on the road to ruin?' I growled. 'Piss off.'

He turned back and rejoined his mates. I wondered if they'd all been betrayed by the same woman.

I went in a corner cafe and had a five-star breakfast and three cups of tea and a smoke and a read of the *Mirror*. The front page was full of grim warnings and a beauty queen. The football pages had the usual attractions, angry managers lashing out, big stars lashing back, gates falling, transfer fees rocketing. West Ham were improving, though. What the hell had gone wrong with my life since I was a kid in the chicken run at Upton Park?

It doesn't do to dwell. The drizzle didn't have the energy to make it into rain and it stopped so I finished my fag. Only one packet of duty-frees left. I couldn't decide if I was clever to have made it this far or just too much of a dumbo to recognize the truth.

I went up Great Chapel Street into Oxford Street.

The cardboard boxes had gone.

Where they'd been was a red milk crate, the plastic kind. On top of it was a small cardboard box.

This had to mean that the three-card trick mob were about.

They didn't show until just before twelve.

Chapter Seven

First off I spotted the dog-eye.

He was a dark-haired, solid-looking bloke standing on the corner of Wardour Street with his hands in his sky-rockets.

You ever seen a man who can look in four directions at once? That's a dog-eye. The three-carders work Oxford Street because it only takes two of these sentries to cover all approaches; the side streets go off at right angles and there are no little alleys or back passages for the Old Bill to creep up unannounced.

This one had the shoulder twitches. I shouldn't be surprised if he thought he looked like Robert Mitchum.

About thirty yards farther on I saw the little knot of men. As I came up they were just beginning to gather a crowd. The dealer was a little bald geezer. He had a fresh, pinkish face and bright blue eyes.

Phyllis Locke had described him to a T. A cheeky little joker.

He was dealing as I strolled slowly past, two cards in his left hand and one in his right. He showed them face-up to the semi-circle of men and then dropped them on the cardboard box, which was standing on top of the up-ended milk crate.

A blind man could have seen the queen – but that's the idea.

One of the men shot out a hand, put a finger on the middle card and slapped down a fiver. The little bald dealer turned over the queen and handed the bloke a fiver.

They all made loud remarks and slapped him on the back. Three or four passers-by drifted in to see what all the excitement was about.

To the passing sucker it looked like free money day.

I strolled past, not wanting to make myself too conspicuous at this stage.

The one who'd copped the five quid was a big blond ugly with a pock-marked face.

They were my men all right.

If it was all down to quickness of the eye against the dealer's skill the three-card game would still be a trap for mugs.

I have seen it done by a lone operator, a wizard whose melody lingers could make cards stand on end and do backsprings. He had to pay out maybe once in a hundred goes.

These guys wouldn't have been happy with odds like that. They have to win every time.

There were seven of them in this team – The Dealer, the two dog-eyes on the corners, and the four heavies round the milk crate. They were the moody audience, the ones who let the whole street know this was where to cop easy money.

How anybody couldn't spot them for baddies beats me. The big one with the pock-marks was only average ugly. One had a face so red and raw it looked as if he always shaved off the top layer of skin.

Another one had an eye condition; the lower lids were so droopy they were almost turned inside out, showing a lot of red eyeball.

The fourth was the youngest. From the look of his face he was struggling to live through the worst hangover since Babylon.

These horrible four were also the minders. First they egged you on by making a big show of winning – all of it the firm's own money – and telling you how easy it was.

That was them being subtle.

If you complained afterwards they were the same four who'd give you a quick boot in the Niagara Falls.

I went to the corner of Dean Street and then came back. There was a crowd round the Dealer now. I looked over shoulders, careful to catch nobody's eye.

One of the plants, the red-faced one wearing a thick navy coat, put his hand on a card.

At this stage the dealer doesn't look too clever and everybody in the crowd knows which card is the queen.

As the red-faced bloke was feeling in his hip-pocket for cash he asked a man standing beside him to put a hand on the card in case the Dealer switched it.

This man was with his wife. They looked like provincials up in town for a day's shopping, real carrot-crunchers.

The husband thought it was great fun and shared a giggle with his wife, putting his index finger on the card.

Red Face pulled out four fivers and whacked them on the card, telling the husband this was easy meat.

Dealer turned the card. Sure enough, the queen. Dealer handed over four fivers to Red Face. The country couple giggled at each other but this time their eyes were asking questions.

Dealer threw down the cards again. Red Face repeated the act, getting the husband to finger the card while he fished for cash. He put down another score. At the same time he was nudging the husband.

'It's easy,' he said loudly, 'you wanna git some of this for yourself – go on, fill yer boots.'

Dealer looked on patiently. Big Blondie with the pock-marks had moved round to that side and was geeing up the wife.

I've seen it all a hundred times and I still had a quick thought that I could bung down a jacks and pick up an easy five.

I didn't.

Red Face won again. They went into the ritual for a third go. This time the husband took the hook. Easy pickings, wasn't it? He got out his notes and his hand stretched out beside Red Face's hand. The dealer had shown them the cards face up and then dropped them, no fancy stuff at all. The queen had to be the card on the right. Our country cousin had twenty quid on it. He and his wife winked at each other, already planning for bubbly at the Hilton Rooftop.

Dealer turned them over.

Six of hearts?

The husband's mouth fell open. How could that be? He started to say something. He'd *seen* the dealer put the queen there. So had this other bloke beside him, the one who'd been doing all the winning.

Red Face shook his head, frowning.

'Sorry, mate, I must of made a ricket there,' he said. 'We'll git him next time – come on.'

The wife pulled her husband away, both of them looking sick.

This routine had taken about five minutes.

Knowing how cute these blokes are I moved away and stood in a doorway ten yards or so along the pavement, pretending to be studying the latest fashions from Harry Fenton. They played on for about fifteen minutes. I decided the Dealer was my man. Not just because he was smaller – he looked bright enough to listen to a business proposition. Big Blondie was a cert to be handier with his boots than his brainbox.

Then they must have had the office from one of the dog-eyes for suddenly the game broke up. Three of them went one way and two the other.

Dealer was one of the three coming in my direction. I let them pass me, watching them in the window reflection. They strolled on a few yards. Sure enough I saw a uniformed bobby coming along the pavement from the Tottenham Court end.

They turned right into Dean Street. By the time I reached the corner they were turning right again into Fareham Street. I went down Dean Street on the other side.

Suddenly they changed their minds and came back into Dean Street and crossed over to the betting shop. Big Blondie appeared a minute later out of Fareham Street with Red Face, having gone round the block the other way.

They disappeared into the betting shop as well.

I reckoned they'd be in there ten minutes at the least so I took a chance and nipped back into Oxford Street and got across the road to Horne Bros the outfitters.

They'd never had such a quick sale. It was a brown cap, corduroy. I asked the salesman to put it in a carrier-bag. Now I looked like a bloke doing some shopping in the West End on his day off. I was going to be hanging round these blokes for a fair spell and the cap could help to change my appearance. Not a lot but maybe just enough.

It was a long, damp afternoon. I risked joining the crowd round the dealer one more time. That was a classic.

Dealer got behind the milk crate, a foot or so from the wall. The kid-on foursome gathered round and started betting furiously. I suppose they had about sixty quid in jacks for this moody betting. I wondered which one of them was trusted enough to hold this working capital overnight – there wasn't one I would have trusted with an Irish penny in a sauna bath.

In moments the flash of blue fivers brought the sheep to the barbers.

This time Dealer was doing the old switched-card trick. Everybody saw where he dropped the queen but when Red Face or Blondie bent his head to check the money he was bringing out of his hip pocket Dealer quickly switched the queen to the other side.

We all saw this. Of course. We were all meant to wonder how anybody could be mug enough to fall for such a clumsy stroke. But Red Face had ten on where the queen had been.

Big Blondie bunged twenty on to the queen in its new place, winking at everybody.

At the same time his eyes were scanning the faces for a sucker.

This time it was a thin, smallish man in a Gannex raincoat. From his face and gear and whatnot I had him down as a factory worker up for his annual wick-dipping in Soho. I could see he thought he was pretty sharp.

When Blondie told him to get in quick he narrowed his eyes and smirked. Other people were the mugs in this world. He knew better. Nobody would ever catch *him*.

At the other side a punter tried to bet a pound but Dealer put him wise.

'Fiver here minimum, you berk, git out ovvit!'

Just as Phyllis Locke said, he had a proper little joker's face.

I watched him as they got ready to skin the bloke in the Gannex. I found myself frowning.

Didn't I know that fresh little face from somewhere? Fairly recent?

Dealer waited. Blondie gave Gannex a nudge. They'd both seen Dealer switch the queen. They were a couple of smart lads who knew the time of day. Easy money.

Dealer turned them over when he saw Gannex wasn't biting.

Red Face at the other side lost his tenner. He looked round in amazement. Men gave him jeering grins. He was the sucker. They smirked at him, the dum-dum. The biggest smirk belonged to Gannex. He watched his new pal Blondie taking twenty quid from Dealer.

On the next deal Gannex didn't need to be told to put his finger on the switched queen to make sure Big Blondie wasn't cheated. Again Dealer had switched the cards while Red Face was exploring his back pocket.

Gannex gave Big Blondie a crafty wink.

'Git some on for yerself, mate,' growled the big pock-marked heavy, slapping down another score.

Gannex smiled patronizingly.

Again Big Blondie won twenty.

Dealer banged them down a third time. The crowd pressed in close. The four minders kept looking at the faces for signs of bother. Red Face pointed to the queen and twisted his head to look at his money. Dealer shifted the card to the other end.

Big Blondie made urgent signs for Gannex to finger the card while he hauled out more money.

This time Gannex not only put his finger on the card, he fished out his own wallet.

In a flash the other two minders moved in close.

Dealer gave him plenty of time, pretending to be having a row with Red Face. Big Blondie and the other two come-ons started nudging and geeing up Gannex, all of them muttering excitedly that he could make himself a bundle from this dealing berk who was trying to swindle people by moving the cards about.

Gannex flipped open his wallet. Dealer was too busy arguing with Red Face to look at him.

Big Blondie stuck a fist with four fivers on the card.

'Git in quick,' he rasped at Gannex.

Gannex fingered the edge of a note. Looking over shoulders I could see a fair wad of brown tenners in the wallet, probably saved up for his annual fling in the sexpots.

'Git it all on,' the minders were urging him, doing a lot of shouting and waving as if they were trying to help him by confusing Dealer.

I thought I'd seen it all before but this bloke was hypnotized. He'd seen the switch, he was reassured by the twenty quid his new pal Big Blondie had stuck on the same card, he was getting friendly advice from all these impartial bystanders.

'Now's yer chance – screw this rotten berk,' they urged, these helpful men in the street.

He brought out two tenners. Stop now, you twit! He brought out another tenner. His face had on a dreamy smile. They were all at him, nudging his elbow, prodding him on.

'Bung it all down – git yourself a bonus!' roared Big Blondie.

'Yeah, take if off the cheatin' bastard,' growled another.

So Gannex pulled out a fourth and then a fifth tenner. Five cockles! His hand hesitated a fraction – but other hands helped to push it forward on to the card.

'Come on – this gentlemun's made his bet – we wanna see it!' Big Blondie barked at Dealer.

The little bald man with the joker's face looked at the fifty quid in the sucker's hand and the twenty quid in Big Blondie's hand. The gang jeered at him and patted Gannex on the back.

Dealer turned over the card.

It was the three of spades.

Gannex stared at it with big eyes. His mouth fell open.

It wasn't possible! He'd seen the queen go down, he'd seen the clumsy switch. So had all these other men. So had this big blond chap, the one who up till then couldn't lose.

How the hell could that be the three of spades?

'Coh – you was fakkin unlucky there,' said the minder with the exposed eyeballs.

Dealer had the notes out of their hands and out of sight before Gannex could get his jaw back in place.

Big Blondie shook his head.

'I could ov sworn it,' he growled to Gannex.

Our friend the eternal victim didn't faint but he had to swallow a lot to keep breathing. Then he edged out of the crowd and walked away, concussed. The team broke up.

I was about fifteen yards behind Dealer when he and Big Blondie and the one who looked like Mitchum made for the betting-shop.

Gannex came past, still shell-shocked. He'd only lost half a hundred, no doubt he was a cert to have blown it anyway on booze and phoney hostesses pretending to be whores but – this way he'd been totally suckered.

He wouldn't even have a hangover to tell him he'd had a good time.

If he'd ever had illusions he now knew the truth beyond argument – he was a right mug.

He'd be too ashamed to tell anybody the truth and it was going to make him sick for the rest of his life.

Sorry for him? Me?

Sorry for any dumbo who strolls into the West End and thinks he can enjoy an honest game of chance with a few sporting chaps who just happen to enjoy an open-air flutter?

You think I'm a naïve sentimental fool? Like all mugs he'd wanted something for nothing. When you weigh it up, he thought *he* was conning the dealer.

So it wasn't too hard to guess what happened with Mrs Spencer's late. The pompous executive type, aggrieved at his luck, a few large whiskies on board, sees this team of scruffy layabouts and decides to win a few quid off them.

How could common herberts like *them* put anything over a man of his calibre?

Then they'd skinned him, only with him being a toff and an

executive he hadn't just sloped off feeling sick. He decided to fight back – or the scotch decided for him.

Trying to catch them he'd been shoved to the deck but he was bulldog breed and all that. He would nail these bounders if it was the last thing he'd ever do.

I wonder what went through his mind as he overbalanced sideways off the crowded platform in front of the train and realized it was his last thing . . .

They were in the betting shop for half an hour. When they came out it was after four and the light was none too clever. They headed through Soho in a bunch, down Dean Street, left into Carlisle Street and then across Soho Square.

Three old winos were flopping about on a park bench. Before, when they were interrupted by the law, the three-carders had been doing their usual skulking but now they were safe and they had the day's earnings in their bin. They jeered at the three old wrecks and walked on, always making the other people step aside, laughing a lot and reaching out to slap each other on the back.

Dealer seemed to be the star of the outfit, although he was the smallest and the oldest. He was wearing an old grey tweed coat, a scruffy white shirt and shabby suedes but he looked like a little bouncy tycoon. When he opened his mouth the others all listened – and laughed.

Doing business with him wasn't going to be easy but at least he seemed to have a sense of humour. Big Blondie looked like the sort who'd kick a hole in a wall.

They went over Charing Cross Road and down the other pavement. I was crossing well behind them when they turned into a side street. I reached the corner as they were disappearing into a doorway, not bothering to look round.

I got there a few seconds later. They'd already gone up the stairs to the Wardorf Club, the same that cousin Tel tried to drag me to.

The Wardorf was a popular West End rendezvous for the fraternity. Any face you saw there you could reckon was *at it*, as they say, a few real gangsters but mainly small-time thieves and touts.

Hoping they weren't going to make a night of it I parked myself in a doorway a few yards from the corner into Charing Cross Road. I lit a fag and watched the Wardorf entrance and tried to remember where I'd seen the dealer before.

It turned dark. A few yards from me the people milled past in their hundreds, some of them hurrying home to cosy weekends with the television, but most of them just arriving on the goodtime scene, faces eager to get amongst the action, the strip joints, the porn shops, the sex shops, the massage shops (Our Speciality – A Thai Massage!), the walk-up whores, the quid-a-drink clipjoints, the sex cinemas . . . you wonder the three-carders see the population as nothing but mugs on the loose?

Great place for philosophy, a dark doorway off Charing Cross Road on a damp night with numb feet and an empty belly.

Then he showed.

Dealer. I saw his bald skull in the light of the Wardorf door-way. It was about half-past six.

He passed me on the other side of the little street and turned right into Charing Cross Road. I was about twenty yards be-hind, getting ready to look in a book shop or a music shop window if he looked back.

He crossed over at the lights. Just for a moment I thought he was going to shout down a taxi. I got ready to make a dive across the pavement and nail him. Even if I could've grabbed another taxi – you imagine what your average cabbie would say if you told him to follow that cab?

And I wasn't going to lose him now and have to start another big walk on Monday morning.

He didn't try for a taxi. He went up to the corner of Oxford Street. I quickened my walk to get closer, nipping left and right through the crowds. It was just as well I got close, he didn't hang about but slipped quickly down into the Tottenham Court Road tube.

I bunged a two-bob bit in a ticket machine as he was sliding through the mobs. Like a little ferret he was. I didn't see him buying a ticket.

We went down the big escalator and then along the tunnel to the Central Line platforms. I expected him to be going east but he turned left on to the other platform.

I was a few bodies away from him as the train battered along to Oxford Circus. He got out. The stairs were jammed with people, which made it harder to keep him in sight but also gave me good cover.

He went to the Victoria Line platforms. I thought he'd be heading north up Tottenham way but again he surprised me.

I kept well away from him till the silver train stopped. He went into the carriage at the double doors. I followed a couple of men in at the single door. He came through the mob in the middle of the carriage and stood in the gangway between the seats. His little cheery face inspected all the people sitting down. Then he hung on a strap.

I got my shoulder against the glass partition and didn't give a view of my face. Occasionally I risked a sideways glance. He was picking his teeth with something and reading the adverts. In those crowds you'd never have given him two looks – he was just little Mr Average, one of the faceless working herberts, a little bald geezer in a soiled white shirt and a shabby tweed coat.

One thing I did notice – he kept brushing his sleeves and front with his left hand, frowning slightly as if he thought he'd been contaminated by the sweaty masses.

We got out at Victoria. Coming up into the big hall he was fifteen yards ahead of me. I went to the automatic gate with my yellow ticket. He had to deal with the collector. I saw him holding out money.

'From Green Park, myte?' the collector was saying, 'that's five, innit?'

'Cheers,' said Dealer.

The little hound! As if skinning mugs all day wasn't enough he'd just diddled London Transport out of a bob.

Of course everybody knows your actual fare-dodgers aren't little working fellas but long-haired economics students and

Persian matrons with six hundred quid in their handbags going home from a hard day's shop-lifting.

At the top of the stairs I bought a *News* and let him pass me. The main rush-hour was over and the crowds were down to a mere avalanche. I followed him across Vauxhall Bridge Road into Victoria Street.

He got in a short queue at a bus stop. I stood at a shop window with the paper up. A couple of buses stopped but he didn't make a move. Then a number 39 arrived, with Putney Bridge on the front.

He nipped up the stairs. I got inside and sat on the first front-facing seat, the ones at the door being too risky.

Not knowing how far he was going I asked the black conductress for a ten. The bus was fairly full. A woman with a silk headscarf knotted under her chin got on in Pimlico Road and sat beside me. She was the Horse and Hound type, or so she wanted us to think, all tweeds and donchyou knows.

Every time the bus stopped I had a quick glance behind to see if the Dealer was on the platform. She kept looking at me resentfully. Maybe she reckoned I was taking up too much of the seat. Or maybe she thought I was after her pommel.

We were going over Battersea Bridge when Dealer came down the stairs. I waited till the driver was slowing into the stop before I put my hand on the rail of the seat in front and said to the tweedy lady:

'Scuse me, luv.'

'Ayyow – jost a mowment,' she neighed.

As she started to rise she dropped a carrier-bag. Half out of the seat she bent down to pick it up, at the time reversing her saddle-end into the gangway to let me out.

It's these damned Labour governments, taxing them so hard they have to use public transport, donchyou know?

I lifted my foot over the seat and did a little vault to escape. I dropped off the platform as the bus was starting away again. I immediately crossed the road to the opposite side from Dealer.

He was walking steadily with his coat collar turned up. All

the years of ducking and diving from the Old Bill had given him a jaunty little step for a bloke of his age.

He went up Parkgate Street and turned right. That's a mixed area that part of Battersea just across the river from Chelsea, high-rise blocks and old terraces and one or two biggish houses standing in their own gardens. I hoped he wasn't going to lose me in a high-rise.

He crossed Rosenau Street. There weren't too many people about it being a cold night so I had to hang back.

He went to the second house from the end of a little terraced row. He had his own key. The house had three floors, no basement. There was a light in the front downstairs room but all the other windows were dark.

I watched to see if any of them would light up. Nothing.

I gave him twenty minutes, in case he was only visiting. Then my feet started to freeze. The hell with it, I thought, steam in.

I pushed open a little wooden gate and went up to the front door. I thumbed the only button. For a few moments all I could hear was the theme music from that television nonsense *Crossroads*, the one set in a Birmingham motel with all the behind the scenes intrigue.

Then the transom window lit up – and I heard these terrible scraping sounds.

They were awful – metal on wood. For half a second I thought they were making barricades with iron bedsteads.

Then the door opened. He was on two sticks and his legs were twisted and when he opened his mouth his eyes almost disappeared as he tried to force a sound out.

'He in?' I said. 'Tell him it's Jim to see him.'

The spastic man made a lot of growling noises. It took me a few moments to catch on to what he was saying. Every word was an effort for him, his whole body was distorted and shaking. But I got on his wavelength eventually. He was telling me he didn't know if Mr Collins was in his room but I could go upstairs and see if I was a friend of his. I had to ask him a couple of times before I was sure he was saying Collins and not Conn or King.

I passed him sideways in the narrow lobby. As I went up the stairs I heard his boots scraping back along the floor to his room.

I knocked on the closed door off the first floor landing. There was another door but it was the carsi.

No answer. Maybe he thought it was a sound effect from *Crossroads*. They do a lot of knocking on doors in that show, any time I've been exposed to it. Gives them something to do with their hands, I expect.

I tried the handle. Locked. I gave it a good thumping. Either he didn't like visitors or he'd broken the world speed record for falling into deep comas.

I took a chance and nipped up to the top floor. There were three small rooms up there, no curtains on the windows, nothing much but junk in any of them. I went back down.

I crouched at the keyhole but it wasn't much of a view, being a Yale lock.

'I'm a friend, I got some money for you,' I said loudly, cocking my ear against a door panel. Not a whisper. I'd have kicked the door in only the chap downstairs might have reckoned that was going in a bit strong, for a friend, on a casual visit.

I went back down. He called me into his room. He had one of those old TV sets with a sheet of magnifying glass strapped over the picture to make it bigger. Most of the room was taken up by a big table. From the amount of stuff on it I should think he near enough lived at that table.

Sitting at it, with his legs out of sight, he looked quite normal – until he started to speak. He was a big man, too, you could see how strong his hands would have been if they hadn't been lop-sided and shaky.

It wasn't the easiest conversation I've ever had but once I got the hang of his voice we got on all right. His name was Pratt. Collins did jobbing contracts of some kind and kept the room for when he was in London for the odd night, mainly at weekends. He'd been renting the room since just before Christmas. I said I'd called on the off-chance of getting some money

Collins owed me. I said he was known as a slippery sam when it came to paying up. We both laughed at that.

He said my best bet would be first thing on Monday morning – Collins usually settled his rent then.

I said okay, only would he mind not telling Collins I'd called as the little rascal might scarper rather than pay me the eight quid he was owing.

Mr Pratt said he wouldn't mind. Collins had been a bit of a disappointment as a lodger, he said. Since his Mum had died he'd been living there on his tod, just the odd lodger to keep him company. Collins was hardly ever there and never had time for a cup of tea and a chat.

He came to see me out. I asked him if he had much of a garden at the back, nodding up the corridor. He said no, it was just a dump out there, he'd had the backdoor nailed up against burglars.

'Thanks a lot,' I said at the door.

'Cheers,' he said, although it didn't sound like that.

I closed his front door and walked away as far as Albert Bridge Road and then came back.

The side street at the end of the terraced row wasn't too well-lit but once I started peering over walls I could see the back yards from the window lights. There was a six foot wall running between the yard of the last house and the pavement but where that wall ended farther up the side street there was a lower wall in front of a house that'd been converted into a builder's office.

From there I could see that the wall running along the bottom end of the yards was half down.

The houses themselves were that old-fashioned kind with the ground-floor coming out in an extension, giving the first-floor a flat roof for sunbathing or growing plants or drying the washing. I couldn't see any light in what I worked out was Collins' window.

I took a quick look in each direction, saw nobody, then vaulted into the builder's yard and walked quickly to a gap in the other wall.

There was enough light from the rear windows to pick my way across the bricks and rubbish in the yard. I got to the extension. It was Mr Pratt's kitchen. Through it I could see the blue light from his TV.

It soon became easier to believe that Collins had skedaddled out the back way. From the side of the extension there was a flight of wooden stairs up to the flat roof.

I started up the stairs. Any noise I made was no match for the combined efforts of all the street's televisions. It was after eight and the nation was either laughing itself to death mechanically or waiting breathlessly for something fatal to happen to Alan Ladd, like a change of expression.

The window of Collins' room was actually a door, two doors really, opening in the middle. Doors with glass – I suppose you'd call them french windows. In Battersea? That's what they were anyway.

Cupping my hands round my eyes I put nose to glass. I could see a fold of curtain but no light. I ran my fingers over the door frame but there was no handle on the outside.

Knowing how shaky these french windows often are I gave the middle part a nudge with my shoulder, not expecting it to give that easily but feeling I ought to try something after getting this far.

The obvious way in was to scrape out the putty and pull out a glass pane but that would warn him somebody was interested. I was undecided what to do next – then the doors gave.

I pushed harder. Something was being shoved across the floor, some heavy weight. Naturally my first thought was – a body! Collins was dead!

For a moment I stood dead still, one foot into the room, trying to remember if I'd put any fingerprints on the glass.

The curtain brushed on my face. I pulled it to one side. There's a trick for seeing things in the dark – don't look directly at what you want to see but a few inches to the side. For some reason things stand out better in peripheral vision.

I saw the vague outlines of furniture. Nothing moved.

I stepped across the door ledge and felt my way across the

room, round a table, across a rug, keeping my fists clenched against fingerprints.

My knuckles found the door and then I stroked the walls for a bit with the backs of my hands, until I hit the light switch.

It was an ordinary room, small, pretty poor, pretty cold. I looked back at the french windows. The 'body' on the floor was an old television set.

I went over to it. There was a thin rope tied round it. The end of the rope was outside on the flat roof. The linoleum was well scratched.

Elementary, Watson. He couldn't lock those french windows on the outside so when he left that way he pulled the rope until the set was tight against the door on the inside, keeping it closed against wind and rain and burglars' eyes.

But why would he want to leave the back way?

One ear cocked for warning footsteps I had a swift gander round the room. There was a single bed, a formica-topped table, an easy chair, two upright chairs, a walnut wardrobe, a small gas cooker with a grille but no oven, a sink with a dish-rack and a chest of drawers. On a little shelf above the sink there was a safety razor, an Aerosol can of shaving soap, a toothbrush, a glass bottle of Old Spice, a plastic packet of Wilkinson Sword Edge showing the card that says you have only one blade left – and a stick of roll-on male deodorant.

A nice blue towel as well.

Did all this good gear belong to that scruffy little hound?

For a moment I couldn't put my finger on what else was curious about that room. Then it dawned. Apart from the washing-stuff there was nothing personal on show, no photographs, no newspapers, no knick-knacks, nothing.

I looked through the chest of drawers. They were empty but for a set of underpants and vest still in Marks and Sparks wrappings and a new pair of black socks still in the sticky band.

Beside the bed there was a pair of dusty suedes. They looked like they'd been dropped in a hurry.

I lifted the pillow. No pyjamas. I went across to the cooker.

No tins of food. The frying pan and two small pots were clean and dry. I turned on a gas tap but nothing happened.

I tried the gas fire in the old fire-place. There was no hiss of gas.

I looked in the wardrobe.

A pair of scruffy trousers on a hanger, a soiled white shirt on a hook, a pair of discarded socks, a set of used underwear, a greasy tie on a string.

I turned the hanger to get at the trouser pockets.

That was when I saw the head of silvery hair.

I cannot tell a lie, I almost yelped with fright.

A man's head – at the bottom of a wardrobe? Battles have been lost over a lot less.

Only it wasn't a man's head, of course. It was a wig on a wooden block shaped like a man's head.

A silvery wig?

No. It *couldn't* be the same man. Collins the Dealer, the scruffy little three-card merchant?

I knew now where I'd seen him before but that was bleeding impossible!

Chapter Eight

I got outside, pulled the TV set up to the french windows and went down the wooden stairs. I got a bus back to Victoria and then the Victoria Line to Oxford Circus. It was almost nine o'clock when I got back to the car in Soho Square.

For a wonder it hadn't been towed away. There were two tickets under the wiper. They joined their mates on the back seat. I drove back to Ravenscourt Park, stopping at a Chinese take-away.

Back in the flat I scoffed three tinfoil plates of sweet and sour pork and then rang Mrs Spencer. Jackie never let me have just the sweet and sour in Chinese restaurants, she said it was too silly without vegetables or anything.

Isn't freedom grand?

'That's wonderful,' said Mrs Spencer when I told her I'd found them.

'I haven't spoken to him yet,' I said. 'I followed him home to Battersea but he skedaddled out the back way. He's a very slippery customer. I'm hoping to nab him on Monday morning.'

'But can we trust him – a man like that?'

'Of course we can't trust him – but he doesn't get the lolly till after the inquest, does he?'

'What if he won't agree to attend the inquest?'

'I'll say Mrs Locke has changed her mind about giving evidence and if he don't play ball with us we'll go to the Old Bill and he'll get all the aggravation without any pay-off. Two hundred quid does a lot of persuading in those circles. By the way, talking about money –'

'Yes?'

'That hundred you paid me – I've done four solid days, Mrs

74

Spencer, Monday will use the hundred up. Maybe if I dropped over your place Tuesday morning – I'll need a few readies to bung this bloke anyway, we'll give him twenty-five to show him we're for real. If you'll give me your address –'

'No, there's no need to come out here,' she said quickly. 'I'm coming into town anyway.'

'Okay, I'm in Fitch's old office. The phone's in the book under his name. Better if I ring you Monday, I don't know where that little shyster will take me next.'

Saturday I went into the office early and got the fridge wired up and plugged in. I went out and bought a couple of bottles of milk and sat there for a bit listening to the whirring while my tipple got cold.

Very pleasant – but not enough to kill a whole Saturday.

I don't normally like that expression about killing time, it's dying fast enough without our help, but I was so curious about Collins the Dealer I could hardly wait for Monday morning.

He was a nothing, Collins, not even a proper villain, just scum, a street rat.

So how in the name of hell could he be the same man I thought he was?

I went out east in the afternoon and saw West Ham against Sheffield United. Hammers did enough to win ten games and let Sheffield get the equalizer with three minutes to go.

Tell me the old, old story.

Coming out with the crowd at time-up I saw Danny Mayes standing with a couple of his mates on the edge of the big fore-court under the main stand. I'd known him from school.

I pushed over that way and said hullo.

Danny put on a funny face at the sight of me. Not funny ha ha, funny peculiar.

'Jim Hazell pon my life,' he said slowly, 'ain't seen you in donkeys. All right are yer?'

'Top of the bill. You?'

'Same as ever. Mustn't grumble. Bin hidin' out, have yer?'

He nodded at me for his friends' benefit. 'Jim here's the same bloke wot saved Keith O'Rourke from a lingerin' old age.'

They both looked at me sharply.

For a moment I thought they might be cousins of Keith O'Rourke, the bloke I'd killed, but no. They'd heard all about it though. We chatted for a couple of minutes. Danny didn't say the obvious about going for a drink.

'Be off then,' I said.

'Cheers,' said Danny. The other two just stared.

As I reached the car in Mafeking Avenue off Barking Road I was kicking myself for speaking to Danny Mayes.

Keith O'Rourke had come after me with a shotgun a year or so earlier and I'd killed him in self-defence. I even had a witness. The police had nothing to charge me with. I'd almost made myself forget the whole deal.

But these blokes had looked at me like I was a leper. They knew the whole story – London's only a big, impersonal place if you're a stranger. Danny Mayes hadn't asked me for a drink because I was healthier not to be with.

Those were blokes who'd been stealing from the docks for generations. At it? They'd offer to flog you a bent lorry and tell you it was a fallen-off-a-lorry lorry.

But killing a bloke – that was a bit strong.

Half an hour later, sitting in an Indian restaurant in Aldgate, I told myself I was stupid. If people were still talking about O'Rourke that was their hard lines for having such dull empty lives.

I'd made my choice and killed him instead of just wounding him because I knew I could get away with it and never be bothered by him again. There was nothing I could do about it now.

Anyway, these blokes had only been curious. It's not everybody who's actually turned another human being off.

Saturday night I washed the other pair of socks. That took

me to about nine o'clock. In my year with Dot I'd hardly ever had time to think of buying record-players or do-it-yourself kits or stamp albums or any of the other things that make for a full life. So what else, I put on the vision. The BBC was *Ironside*, ITV was all those mimics, BBC-2 was some arty deal about women dressed in Greek togas and shouting about death, I dunno.

I found the paperback of Papillon and left on *Ironside* just to keep me company until the football. Great Saturday night. I fell asleep and when I came to it way past close-down, just a pinpoint light in the centre of the screen and a strong buzzing from the set.

When I went to bed I couldn't get to bleeding sleep. Why the hell did I have to meet Danny Mayes and start thinking about Keith O'Rourke again?

Sunday I went over to see Mum and Dad at Haggerston. When Mum went out to start the dinner I asked Fred if he'd heard anything lately about the O'Rourkes.

'We ain't hearin' nuffin from Keef, that's a cert,' he growled cheerily. Keith's younger brother had been in the team that did for Fred's legs and he was well proud of me for having shot the bastard dead.

'What about the rest of them?' I said.

'Alan's about due back from bein' away,' he said. Away meant Chelmsford nick. 'Don't worry about him, no bottle has he?'

'Only I met Danny Mayes over at West Ham yesterday and from what he was saying I thought maybe the O'Rourkes might be telling people I was down for a seeing-to.'

'Worried about that lot ov bums, are yer? Most of the people fink you done a good job wiv Keef. Here – wot you remember from school about the Duke of Wellington?' He shoved a paper-back at my face and then pulled it back quickly when I tried to take it. 'You buy yer own,' he said.

I told them about my Mayfair office at dinner. At home what we have in the middle of the day is dinner. They were impressed by Mayfair. Dad wanted to know how many times I'd been round the Duke of Wellington's house.

'Leave it out,' I moaned. Since he'd been done over by Alan O'Rourke and his team in the betting-shop raid he'd been as good as crippled and reading had become his number one hobby after the telly.

Like most who take up reading late in life he wanted to educate you from the book he was currently enjoying. He did, however, manage to give the Duke of bleeding Wellington a rest for the football on television. I had a second chance to see West Ham throwing away their lead to Sheffield United.

It hadn't been all that clever a game the day before but the ITV commentator made the edited version more thrilling than England winning the World Cup.

During the adverts I asked the old man if he'd ever run across a three-card trick merchant called Collins, a little bald geezer about fifty. In a city of eight million you might think it was pretty long odds against him knowing Dealer but we're not talking about the whole population. In those circles you get to know most of the names, if you live long enough.

My old man was never a proper villain, not really.

'Collins? Wot's his first name?'

'Dunno.'

'Can't help yer, sorry. Three-card trick mob? I wouldn't know people like them, would I? Scum they are, fakkin scum. Is that wot you're workin' amongst now, is it? Bit ovva come-down innit, wiv an offis in Mayfair? You take a real worker – one ov the fanny mob or a cracksman or even a dip, anybody wiv a bit ov class, he'll tell yer – three-card trick? They ain't got the brains to blag their way into proper con tricks and they ain't got enuff bottle just to smash people on the head. Here – I got somethin' better for yer. *He's* offerin' five grand reward, innee?'

'Who is?'

'Billy Bunter Begg a course! You ain't heard nuffink about him? Nah well, you wouldn't would yer, not hangin' about *Mayfair*. Got his own firm. Up Walthamstow he works from.

Supposed to be a builder's merchant only he's a gangster.'

'Why don't they arrest him then?' asked my Mum, no doubt glad of a change from football and the Duke.

'Arrest him? Wot's got into you, woman?' roared the old man. 'It ain't a crime to be a gangster – they gotta catch yer doin' somethin', anney?'

'So what's the five grand reward all about?' I asked, waving away my Mum's plate of cake. Cake? After all that chicken and roast potatoes? I sometimes wonder if she isn't trying to fatten people up for something.

'Some hero has had it away with ninety grand ov Billy's money,' said my Dad. 'He's doin' his nut by all accounts. Fred Petchey told me, he's well in wiv Begg's brovver-in-law Tommy Trott. It was his life savin's, wunnit? Half-inched from his safe deposit 'cordin' to Petchey. An' nuffink he can do about it cos he's niver paid tax on it!'

'Don't you be having nothing to do with a man like that Begg,' my Mum said, trying to pour me some more tea.

'Bleedin' hell, woman,' growled the old man, 'he's a private detective, innee? Wot you want, he's only gotta take safe jobs, down the Boy Scout hut sussin' out who nicked the cocoa tin?'

'Don't worry,' I said, 'I'm not tangling with any heavies. Is he paying five grand for the money back? Got a bit of a hope, hasn't he? If I find his ninety grand I trot round to him with it and he gives me five?'

'Nah – for information – how did ninety grand take a stroll from a safe deposit box? No break-ins or nuffink.'

'Sounds like the perfect crime.'

'If you kin git away wiv it. He's not supposed to be too bad a sort, Begg, but I hear he's shot off his fair share ov kneecaps. Rather than his ninety grand I'll have poverty this side ov the coffin lid.'

I stayed at Haggerston till the end of *Colombo*. I suppose an outsider would have marked us down a typical square-eyed family. So what? Where's the harm? It's just the same as sitting round the old coal fire.

Not so easy to do the toast, though.

I was back in Rosenau Street by seven on Monday morning, parked opposite the side street so I could see the front door of the house and the builder's wall.

It was dry but cold with a blue sky. That part of Battersea is very pleasant, the mixed-up buildings and lots of trees and not too much traffic. The toffs are already trying to move in and call it south Chelsea. Yellow doors and working folks' houses costing ten times over the odds – the kiss of death.

A milkman was carrying bottles from a green Co-op float. A West Indian woman came out to her gate and shouted something. The milkman waved and went back for a box of eggs from the coldbox.

A young bloke with long hair and a gas mask case came out of another house pushing a bike. I think they're handing them down father to son, those gas mask bags. Surely nobody's making new ones?

Men went to work.

Children yelled. Housewives stopped for a natter over the railings. It looked like a simple, lovable world.

I was slumped down in the driver's seat, my back against the door, my feet pushing against the other door. I had the window open an inch to let the smoke out. After a whole Sunday of my Mum's feeding I wasn't going to be hungry till Wednesday.

He showed just before eight. He was coming up the side street from Albert Bridge Road, walking slowly and reading a newspaper. He looked like a bloke who'd nipped out for a paper – but he hadn't come out of the house, front or back.

As he came opposite me I saw he was wearing dark blue trousers and shiny black shoes under the same old tweed coat. He had a blue scarf round his neck.

He went in the front door. I gave him five minutes. I was pretty sure he was only using that room for changing, which meant I still had to find his real gaff.

In no time at all he reappeared at the front door. A casual look and you wouldn't have thought there was any difference but he had changed back into the scruffy old trousers, the dusty suedes, the soiled white shirt.

He came down to the gate and looked up and down the street. I kept my head well down. We were about forty yards apart. He brought something out of his pocket. I couldn't see what it was but I recognized the hand movements.

I heard Kevin Barclay's hooray voice . . . *he picks his teeth, you know, breaks matches and uses the jagged ends . . .*

It was him all right. The wig in the wardrobe had put me on to the possibility but I had no doubt now. Collins the Dealer was Simon Coddington from the SS *Apollo*!

It was an amazing coincidence but there you go. Who better to work a casino fiddle than a street card-sharp?

The only bit that puzzled me was the cruise ticket. At eight hundred that meant they had to chop well over a grand out of the casino before they got into profit. It seemed a lot.

I was entitled to be puzzled. Collins the Dealer alias Coddington was only just starting to show me his bag of tricks.

Chapter Nine

He walked down the side street. I got out, ready to follow him to Oxford Street, seeing another day's lurking ahead of me.

But it was worth it now. I could get him for the casino fiddle and cut myself in for a fair whack of Dot's fee. He was bound to lead me to the girl, sooner or later. Then I'd dive in.

He wasn't going for a bus.

Just before he reached Albert Bridge Road he stopped beside a green Thames van and fished in his pockets.

I turned quickly back to the Stag. I was swinging into Parkgate Street when the green van was disappearing into Albert Bridge Road. There was only a Cortina between us as we reached Albert Bridge. He turned right on to the Embankment.

Two solid lanes of morning rush hour traffic were moving in a jerky crawl, the occasional spurt only increasing the frustration.

I wasn't brimming over about the way this had turned out. Tailing another motor looks dandy in films but in the real it's diabolical, if not impossible. Even when I was on the Squad and we had three or four cars with experienced drivers working together on the radio we'd reckon to lose the quarry eight times out of ten.

My only chance was that he didn't expect to be followed.

We rolled past the grounds of the Royal Hospital. No Chelsea Pensioners in sight. He turned left at Chelsea Bridge Road. Only a two minute drive but we'd left that scruffy little part of Battersea far behind. London's like that, the poor and the rich living two yards from each other but never crossing the invisible barriers.

Not that I'm against some people having big houses and plenty of money. Not at all.

Why does it always have to be the same people, though?

We went past the Guards barracks and across Pimlico Road into the swank territory of Lower Sloane Street.

He didn't have much rear vision through the small van windows so I kept really close to him.

As ever Sloane Square was fun to get round. Just as you might expect, a Bentley came out of King's Road and stopped bang in front of me, blocking most of the road.

A lady got out, hand-tooled skin and all the time in the world. She lifted some parcels out of the back seat. It wasn't half-past eight so she couldn't have been shopping. Probably she was bringing back last week's impulses for a refund.

She gave her driver detailed orders to cover every minute of the day ahead and then sauntered to the pavement. She looked round with an innocent face, wondering why all these common people were scaring the starlings out of the trees with their damned hooters.

I'd seen the green van go into the top part of Sloane Street at the theatre end of the square. I did some aggressive stuff to catch up.

We were about a dozen vehicles apart as he turned left into Grosvenor Place towards Hyde Park, the Queen's garden wall across the street on our right.

Hyde Park Corner was a sea of windscreens and grim faces. Filtering they call it, hundreds of stomach linings twisting into ulcers.

He got into Park Lane for the race up to Marble Arch. My problem here was to stop myself overtaking him, the van only managing about forty top whack. I got into the inside lane and hoped he wouldn't look back.

Hyde Park was very green in the sun, all that clear morning air and the trees beginning to bud. A paunchy executive in a blue track suit was jogging along the path, no doubt imagining himself on his Olympic come-back. A tall lady in white trousers and a sailor's jacket and a cute little yachting cap was walking two white borzois.

Life looked grand over there.

Marble Arch was another filtering foul-up, cars coming in all directions and getting jammed door-to-door never mind bumper-to-bumper.

A motor-cycle cop was out in the middle, holding up two lanes from Bayswater Road to let the roundabout stuff through to Edgware Road or Oxford Street. I saw him looking over the roofs and then raising his arm to point at the car he wanted to stop.

Did he mean me?

Maybe he did.

Collins went into Oxford Street, then turned left at Portman Street. He went straight up Gloucester Place and across Marylebone Road.

Next thing we were in Prince Albert Road, the one that runs round the north side of Regents Park, passing the Armstrong-Jones' birdcage and the Zoo gates.

Then Parkway to Camden Road. We passed the Medical Rehabilitation Centre where I'd gone to have remedial exercises for my ankle. The exercises were to music and I felt like a right nana and now I wished I'd stuck the whole course.

More invisible barriers. One minute the luxury penthouse balconies overlooking Regents Park, the next we're sliding into sight of Holloway women's prison.

For a moment I thought Collins might be visiting a wife or something but he drove on down Parkhurst Road.

A big sign said:

ROAD WORKS AHEAD.

I hoped it would.

Finsbury Park was where tailing him became tricky. Most of the traffic was coming into London at that time in the morning. I began to feel conspicuous but I couldn't hang too far back in case he lost me at the Manor House junction.

He went straight over and along Seven Sisters Road, the green van toddling along at a steady forty, no sign of him trying to shake me.

I knew that bit of Seven Sisters Road well from years ago. Manor House was the tube station we got out at on Saturdays going to see Spurs play.

You could always get a special bus to White Hart Lane but never one back. As a boy, walking back along that road of big council flats, I used to pray for it to come to an end.

That was when Danny Blanchflower and Tommy Harmer were the Spurs geniuses. Where did it all go, eh?

He slowed down in the outside lane at the Amhurst Park turning. We were the only vehicles going north. I couldn't risk drawing in behind him for the right turn so I kept on down the hill and then did a swift u-turn.

He was out of sight when I got back up to the corner. I turned left and saw him about fifty yards ahead. We were now in Stamford Hill, Borough of Hackney. A red light stopped him at the High Road crossing. I knew that part quite well, the secondhand car place on one corner, the big cinema now empty and disused on the other, an orthodox Jew with a little skull cap and a big beard on the pavement.

The lights changed. There was a laundry van between us. We went over the High Road and down past the little stretch of park called Clapton Common.

I'd been pushing my luck all the way from Battersea but when he turned left into Spring Hill, the road at the bottom end of the park, I was in dead trouble.

It was the first time we'd been off main roads. I slowed down and cruised after him at about twenty.

He took the first left. I dawdled up to the corner. Overlea Road it was called. I nosed forward until I could see up the length of it. He was getting out of the van, locking it up. I reversed quickly and parked. When I got back to the corner on foot he had gone.

It was a quiet little street, suburban, you'd call it, two-storey houses with those rounded porthole windows, privet hedges, little lawns, wooden railings most painted white or green.

Quiet, too.

So what did I do now?

I picked a house at this end. It had a lightweight knocker above the letterbox. I gave it a polite tap or two.

Inside the house a dog went spare. I've never got on too well with dogs.

A pleasant smile on my features and my right foot ready to kick this hound in the throat I watched the door open.

It was a teenager of the boy variety, seventeen and less chat than Buster Keaton. He was in bare feet, brushed denim trousers and a sleeveless Fair Isle pullover. It was hardly nine o'clock but he looked dreamy, shoulders still swaying to the latest funky baloney.

How come I never got all that lounging around when I was spotty?

'Sorry to bother you,' I said, 'you don't belong to that green Thames van out there by any chance?'

He turned his head and said something to the dog, which was now busting a gut.

'Do what?' he said, less patiently, to me.

'The green van out there – you know whose is it? Only I just give it a scrape with my motor.'

He stuck his head out far enough to see the van without exposing his tootsies to the cold.

'Not ours,' he said, shaking his head.

'The driver – he a little bald fella?' I said. 'I saw him near it earlier on. Only I don't want to slope off without telling him, do I?'

'Yeah, Copeland, three doors up,' he said, jerking his styling to the left.

'Cheers,' I said, to a closed door. No time to waste, these modern kids.

The dog went on yelping.

I went along the pavement, pushed open an iron gate, went up a little path and pressed a little button.

He didn't open the door very wide. About the distance from ear to nose.

'Mr Copeland?' I said, to half of a bald skull and one eye.

'Who wants him?' he snapped.

Only three little words but there was no doubt about it – this was Coddington from the SS *Apollo*.

I waited for the one eye to remember seeing me before. It just went on staring at me.

'Can I have a word?' I said.

'What d'yer want? Who are yer?'

'I want a word. My name's James Hazell.'

'Wot's your business? I don't buy nuffin at the door.'

'I'm in the enquiry business.'

'Yeah? Well Copeland ain't in. Come back next year.'

'Not in? Cross your heart and hope to die?'

He opened the door wide enough to let me see the rest of his face.

'Look, friend, I told you, din I? Go an' enquiry somewheres else, go on, piss off.'

Thieves and villains are the only ones left who believe an Englishman's home is his castle. His welcome was not particularly hostile by the standards of those circles.

'I still want a word,' I said.

'Stand there all bleedin' day then for all I fakkin care.'

He tried to shut the door but I got my foot in. I couldn't think of anything more subtle to keep us on speaking terms.

'Not very friendly, are we?' I said, showing him my teeth as I held the door open. 'Maybe you'd be more in the mood for a chat in Rosenau Street?'

The pressure slackened on my foot.

'Who the hell are yer?' he growled, cheeky little face screwed into a frown. That close to I saw that he'd started growing a moustache. From the look of it he'd be gone before it struggled into life. He was looking behind him nervously. 'I dunno wot's goin' on – look, I'll meet yer up the street in a couple ov minutes.'

'I don't think so,' I said, raising my voice. He waved his hand about, making sshhing signals. 'I don't want you doing your invisible man stunt out the back way.'

'All right, for God's sake don't tell the whole bleedin' world.' He left the door and then reappeared, pulling on the tweed coat.

No earthly doubt about it.

Simon Coddington!

'Where's yer car?' he hissed as we reached the pavement. 'We can sit in it, only do hurry, I don't want The Enemy knowin' nuffin about this.'

'Your van would be better,' I said, not wanting him to see my car. It was just a precautionary reflex. He didn't argue. Battersea was obviously the magic word. He walked round the front of the van, unlocked the cab driver's door and then let me in.

'Smashing day,' I said.

He stared hard at me. I could hear him wondering if he hadn't seen me before somewhere.

'How d'yer know about Rosenau Street?' he demanded.

'I followed you there on Friday night, didn't I?'

'So how d'yer know about this place?'

'I followed you again this morning.'

'Wot the bleedin' hell for? Tell us for pete's sake, wot's it all about?'

He sounded quite plaintive. I reminded myself how much mercy he'd shown the suckers in Oxford Street.

'The name Spencer mean anything to you, Dad?' I said.

He frowned. He didn't like Dad. He shook his head. Then he switched on the engine.

'Better drive round a bit in case The Enemy clocks us out the front window.'

'Under the cosh are you?'

'Who ain't? Spencer you say? Nah, means nuffin to me.'

'He's a geezer who fell under a train in the Oxo at Tottenham Court Road a week or so ago.'

'Oh yeah – I think I remember readin' somethin' about that. Done himself in, dinnee?'

'No – he was chasing after some three-card trick merchants.'

'That wasn't in the linens.'

'No, it's new evidence. I dug it up myself.'

'Real ferret you must be. Wot's all this gotta do with me then?'

'Slippery to the end, eh?'

He turned right at the end of the little park. There were a few people at a wooded hamburger stand. He parked in Craven Walk. Nice part that.

'All right, we've had the fancy footwork,' I said, rolling down my window and lighting an Embassy. He didn't smoke, he said. I looked at his fingers for nicotine stains. If he'd told me it was cold I'd have started to sweat. 'I followed you to Rosenau Street on Friday night after watching you conning the mugs in Oxford Street. This bloke Spencer, you had a ruck with him and he was chasing after you and fell off the Central Line platform in front of a train. Right?'

'This fairytale have a happy endin', does it?'

'Mrs Spencer is very keen not to have it down to suicide.'

'Yeah? She can't collect from the Pru if it's suicide, that it?' He turned his face towards me and grinned. It *was* Coddington. I still couldn't believe it.

'She's a very sincere church-goer,' I said, 'suicide isn't what they do at all. So that's where you come in.'

'I thought it might be but it ain't.'

'Hear me out first. The lady is willing to offer a reward for information.'

'Smoking's a filthy habit,' he said, disapprovingly.

'All you have to do is tell the inquest on Thursday what happened and that'll prove her husband didn't commit cash and carry.'

'Inquest? Leave me out!' He sounded shocked.

'It's not all that dramatic. You say you had a ruck with him after he lost a few quid guessing queens. He chased you to the tube and you pushed him off but he was still after you – he must have gone to the very edge to get up the platform and missed his footing. Where's the harm in that for you?'

'If I tell you,' he said, raising his hands and shaking his head. 'I swear to God. That is exactly what did happen, to a T. Except that we didn't have nuffin off him.'

'He just didn't like your style, eh? I don't see any harm in admitting you were working the boards.'

'Niver mind all that – you must be fakkin jokin' if you think I'm givin' evidence!'

'The Old Bill can't charge you unless they get you at it. What's the maximum fine anyway – a score? A pony? Even if they did try to get all busy after the inquest Mrs Spencer will pay the onion money. Plus two hundred reward for coming forward with the information.'

'Two hundreds?'

'Not bad for a day's work, is it?'

He stared ahead, a hint of amusement about his eyes. This made me wonder if he had a tool in the van. Not the nuts and bolts kind, the grievous bodily kind. Violence wouldn't be his normal style but my arrival in his life must have been a real choker. I didn't take my eyes off him for a moment.

I'd have needed his neck under a forked stick before I relaxed in his company.

'Nah, I think a monkey's more like,' he said at last. 'Worth that to her, innit?'

'Five hundred? I could always turn the whole deal over to the Old Bill and then you can blow kisses to your readies.'

'Nah, the law can't do nuffin – you ain't got a witness.'

'No? How the hell you think I got on to you in the first instance? Course I got a witness.'

'Yeah? Who for example?'

'Oh sure. I'll give you the address as well. You can send a few chums round to hammer general amnesia into his skull?'

He looked at me carefully. The couple of times we'd been face to face on the *Apollo* he'd been concentrating on Stephanie Parmenter and I'd just been one of the flunkeys in penguin suits.

It was still incredible he didn't recognize me.

'Four hundreds,' he said.

'Uh uh. Two.'

'Four's rock bottom.'

'I hate to be crude but.'

'But wot?'

'Your wife – The Enemy, sorry – she know about your pad

in Rosenau Street? I'd hate to be the one to destroy her illusions.'

'Okay you bastard, two hundreds. Only I gotta better idea. We'll put it all down to Desperate – that's the big geezer wiv the fair hair. He was wiv me, he ain't no Brain of Britain but he could learn to recite your dialogue. I got this phobia like, a psychological block you'd call it – just couldn't be standin' in a court an' *admittin'* things. Dear oh dear. Nah, we'll fit up Desperate for that end ovvit. But you bung me the two tons, right?' He smiled. 'Desperate trusts Uncle Sidney you see.'

'Carve it up any way you fancy long as one of you gets up there and says the necessary.' I gave him his treachery smile back. 'Don't plan anything too slippery, will you? I mean you nause up this deal and The Enemy hears about Mr Collins of Battersea. And that's just for starters, I'm sure I could think up a nice rosy future for you.'

His eyebrows went up in honest amazement.

'You got me by the cream crackers, I ain't likely to cross you, am I?'

'Because I'm a devil when people take liberties with me,' I said, shaking my head and frowning as if puzzled by my own brutality.

'I'll see Desperate tomorrer, you can meet him an' indoctrinate him. Only don't tell him nuffin about the price. Where's your gaff?'

'It's Shepherd Market, Mayfair – one four seven. Ring the top button. What time?'

'About five, give us a chance to do some graftin' first.'

'It always worries me about you bastards – you never feel *any* sympathy for the mugs?'

His smile this time was genuine.

'*Worries* you, do it? People starvin' to death all over the world, little children sufferin', country goin' bankrupt an' you're worried about me takin' a few quid off ov greedy berks who're actually tryin' to take a few quid off ov me? Not *worried*, surely. *Perturbed*, maybe, or mildly *curious* – but not *worried*. Unless you're needin' to see a psychiatrist.'

91

'Save your spiel for Saint Peter.'

'If all the honest people really was honest us lot wouldn't stand a chance, would we?'

He started the van and drove down Craven Walk. He turned right into Ashtead Road and then back up Spring Hill to the end of Overlea Road.

'Your car here?' he said, all innocent.

'Not far,' I said, 'I'll get out here. Don't hang about, The Enemy'll be wondering what's happened to you.'

He laughed.

'It's all a game, innit?'

'See you tomorrow then.'

'Count on it.'

I stood on the pavement and watched him drive up his little suburban type street to his cosy home. I saw him get out of the van and go up his garden path. He looked along the street at me and I gave him a wave. He went into the house.

I moved back against a hedge.

Sure enough he was back at his gate a couple of seconds later. He looked at the cars and didn't see me. I went back round the corner and drove the Stag down Spring Hill, left into Ashtead Road and then back up Craven Walk, parking near enough the little common to see the green van whichever way he came out.

It took him half an hour to make a move. Maybe he was being clever. More likely it took him that long to think up a story for The Enemy.

He came out past the park and turned right into the main road, heading back the way we'd come.

My guess was Rosenau Street. He'd been rumbled and the obvious move was to grab his bits and pieces and abandon that room.

But why was he keeping a room just for changing?

Only one answer. He was obviously leading some kind of secret life his dear wife The Enemy didn't know about. And wherever else he went he had to be wearing good clothes and the wig.

He was Copeland at home in Stamford Hill, Collins at Battersea – so where was he playing Simon Coddington?

It had to be something connected with the casino fiddling.

Which meant a chance for me to pick up some real money, once I'd put the pieces together . . .

I wanted to get there before him so I stepped on it and drove by Stamford Hill High Road, Stoke Newington Road, Balls Pond Road and Essex Road, down to The Angel, Islington, then Pentonville Road to Euston Road, taking on four gallons at a filling station in Marylebone Road, down Park Lane to Hyde Park Corner and then Knightsbridge and Brompton Road to Fulham Road, a left turn at Sydney Street in Chelsea, right into King's Road, left down Oakley Street and over the Albert Bridge – and there I was back in Rosenau Street.

I did it in under half an hour. There was no sign of the van. I parked about ten yards from the corner, diagonally opposite the end of the terraced houses.

He turned up about half-past twelve, just when it looked like I'd won the paper-hat. I was sprawled out on the back seat, my head well down. Nobody ever looks for a tail in the back seat.

He came walking up from Battersea Bridge Road, just a little bald nonentity in a shabby tweed coat. A nobody man you would have said, a joiner maybe or a plumber's mate, a sports page reader.

He went into the house by the front door.

Ten minutes later he came back out. He had a good look round, didn't spot me, shouted something back into the lobby, closed the door and walked round the corner.

Tricky little bastard, he had the van parked in Albert Bridge Road, although he'd approached the house from the other direction. Its near wheels were up on the pavement. He threw in his bundles. The Thames van lurched off the kerb and drove towards the bridge.

I let a couple of cars get past before I came out of the side street. If he saw me this time I wasn't too bothered – I had enough on him to threaten him with The Enemy – but I thought I'd give it a bit of a go.

Over the bridge he turned left into Cheyne Walk, veering right where the Embankment turns away from the river at Lots Road. The traffic was fairly heavy and he didn't have much chance of bursting away.

He turned left into King's Road. I reached back and got the corduroy cap off the back seat and pulled it well down on my forehead. It wasn't much of a disguise but it hid my hair.

He drove on down King's Road into New King's Road and then over Putney Bridge, turning right into Upper Richmond Road. There was enough traffic to keep me anonymous. Most of the other cars were driven by solitary men, sales reps starting out from head office for a week on the road.

Their faces didn't look too hysterical but no doubt they had exciting plans. I felt like waving to them. There's something about a chase, doesn't matter which end of it you're at. You don't have time to worry about the rent.

Then he lost me, just when I was getting in the mood to sing.

We were on Richmond Road, passing through Mortlake. He took a quick left turn. I was about five cars behind.

By the time I reached the side street he was out of sight. I turned off the main road and began to drive round the little streets looking for the green van.

Eventually I spotted it, parked beside a school playground, not a single clue to where he might have gone.

I pulled in a few yards farther up on the same side. The playground was empty. Across on the other side was a row of lock-up garages. I switched off and lit a fag. I supposed he'd have to come back to the van sometimes but I was already feeling hungry.

I was also needing a Jimmy Riddle.

Talk about the dunce's paper-hat? Sitting in a side street in Mortlake, watching an empty green van, stomach rumbling, bladder topping up, feeling like the only Mountie whose man got away?

What happened next would've been an easy one for Thomas to doubt.

One of the lock-up garage doors suddenly went up.

Just like that, nobody near it. As if the Invisible Man had forgotten his bandages.

Out of the shed backed the unmistakable sloping glass rear and double exhaust pipes of a yellow Jensen Interceptor.

It stopped and then went forward and swung out into the street, six or seven grand's worth of prestige motoring.

Out he stepped. Only he was Simon Coddington now, the silvery wig, pale blue shirt, dark tie, blue mohair suit.

It was uncanny. The shabby nonentity had changed to the self-made tycoon. The face was the same but that was all.

He walked diagonally across the street to the van. He passed the Stag less than ten yards away. He didn't even look at it. I was staring him right in the face but he was puzzling over something.

He got into the van, drove it across the road into the open lock-up, came out, pulled down the door, locked up, dusted his hands, walked to the Jensen, got in, started up and shot off.

I did a fast u-turn but I was still fifty yards from the main road when he disappeared left into the westbound traffic.

Up till then he'd been full of surprises but it wasn't too hard to see how Copeland the street con-man could turn himself into Coddington the vulgar little rich man.

Those three-carders can pick up a lot of loot in spasms. He might even have found a way to fiddle a cruise ticket. And anybody can steal good clothes.

But a Jensen Interceptor?

He wasn't making that kind of lolly fleecing suckers on the pavements of Oxford Street.

It had to be a rich woman who'd chosen him for a fancy man I decided.

I was still under-estimating that slippery little bastard.

Chapter Ten

I was lucky on that part of it. He got caught behind a French juggernaut. When he did flash out to overtake his bright yellow paintwork was like a beacon in the night.

I got within a dozen cars of him. The Stag can do a fair turn of speed but he would have lost me easily but for the speed limit. God bless the government for spurning all those maniacs who find life unbearable unless they're passing it at ninety.

Most of all I was lucky because he thought he was dead clever. Maybe all the years of shuffling the mugs out of their lolly had given him a big head. He obviously didn't reckon on anybody being cute enough to be still on his trail.

He was about fifty or sixty yards ahead of me in the fast lane on the Twickenham Road. I kept getting glimpses of yellow through other windscreens. At the big Chertsey Road round-about he went right into St Margaret's Road.

I got caught at the junction for a few moments but when I made the right turn I could see the yellow car taking the first right.

He was out of sight by the time I reached that corner but I turned in anyway. It was a swanky area, long avenues, big hedges, the houses hiding behind leaves of some kind. I stopped and got out the A to Z street map.

There weren't too many of these roads between there and the river. I started to cruise.

I went down Ailsa Road and that took me back to the main road again. I did a u-turn and went back along the quiet avenue, slowing at each gate, peering through gaps in the greenery.

I turned right at St Margaret's Drive and then right again.

Up and down I went. There was enough vegetation about to hide Southend Pier. It's always the same, the quieter the street the more they want to camouflage themselves.

Maybe it's a guilt complex about all that wife-swapping.

Then I saw the flash of yellow. The Jensen was parked just inside the gateway of a square, two-storey, red-brick house with a bit of ivy up the front.

I didn't have a lot of time to study the lay-out. As I came past the gate he was standing at the open boot of the Jensen. He was talking to someone over at the front door.

At that speed I couldn't be certain but the woman he was talking to had all the appearance of Jennifer Carmichael, the luscious girl dealer from Down Under.

That *was* a puzzler.

They were only a couple of smalltime chisellers. Two bent dealers in the same bed? Couldn't trust each other enough for a friendly game of snap.

Just because the people in those posh suburbs don't stand gossiping at the garden gate in vest and braces scratching their armpits doesn't mean they're behind with the news.

Parking the Stag a good bit away, I called at a single-storey house about five gates down from The Beeches. It had such heavy roses round the front you automatically got scratched trying to reach the front door. I pressed a white button.

The door didn't open but a lady came round from the back of the house. She was wearing slacks and gardening gloves. She was coming on for fifty, fairly handsome in a leathery sort of way.

It was the old estate agent trick for her. I was acting for clients whose dream was to live in that part. I was calling on the off-chance somebody might like a quick fortune.

She said her husband would never contemplate leaving this heaven on earth. I said oh. Did she by any chance think any of her neighbours might be amenable to a generous offer?

She was going mad with boredom and asked me in to tea.

I'm not guessing – she told me she was bored. Her children were grown-up, her husband was one of those high-powered executives who absolutely *yearn* to spend more time at home, or so they keep telling their wives on the phone, she didn't have to work, she didn't even have to wash a dish – most of the time, she said, pouring me a cup of tea in a fancy mug, she had to fight down an urge to scream.

My little problem was just the thing to liven up the afternoon so she started giving me the dirt on the neighbours. I said I rather fancied a house about four up, the one with the green roof tiles. She said, funny, the couple who live there were a bit of a talking point, locally.

In fact, people were downright curious. Coddington was *his* name. He'd bought the house in November or early December but *she*, his much younger 'wife', hadn't turned up until a week or so ago.

She was quite definite about it – he'd bought the place. She'd been very close with the Parker-Owens, they'd been selling to retire to Devon. The way the market was they'd been getting quite *frantic*, then this Mr Coddington arrived out of the blue and offered them cash. Yes, cash. They'd been asking forty-two thou. He got it for thirty-seven. Six years ago it was worth about twelve.

The few words Coddington had exchanged with the neighbouring suavos indicated he wasn't from the top drawer. I said tuts tuts, that's the kind of vulgarian who's got the finance these days. She said it wouldn't be so bad if they *were* vulgar and brought some life to the avenue but Coddington was just never there.

She wanted to show me her borders but I said I was on a tight schedule and left with many thanks.

I drove past the house again but the yellow Jensen had been garaged, or he'd left again. I headed back to town.

I knew most of it now but not the most important thing of all. Where the hell had Uncle Sidney got the money?

He'd paid out thirty-seven grand for the house – never mind

the car, the eight-hundred pound cruise, two wigs at probably a hundred each, and the mohair whistle and toot.

You don't make that kind of lolly skinning carrot-crunchers in Oxford Street. You don't even make it chopping into a casino takings.

The first thing for me was find out the price on their heads.

Dot looked up sharply. She'd been talking to a youngish bloke sitting in front of her desk. He looked round. He had one of those cool, well-bred faces. He was wearing a grey overcoat with raglan shoulders, not trendy but dear.

'What the hell's this?' Dot snapped.

'Sorry,' I said, nodding to her visitor, 'if I'd known you had company I would have knocked. I'll wait till –'

'No, it's all right, I'm going anyway,' he said. He had a snob accent but it wasn't quite natural. He stood up. Dot went on glaring at me.

'Get out of here,' she snapped.

'Perfectly all right I assure you,' he said, heading for the door. He smiled at her. He had a smooth complexion and red lips. His hair was medium brown, just long enough to be curling on his collar.

'I'll let you get on with it,' I said, trying to circle round him to get to the door.

'My dear chap! I'm on my way. Nice to have this chat, Miss Wilmington, hope it wasn't a complete waste of your time. Bye.'

He shut the door.

'Sorry, honest,' I said.

'Gimme that key,' she demanded, holding out her hand. I took it off my key-ring and put it on her blotter. 'If I'd known you were coming I'd have changed the lock,' she said.

'I've said sorry so can we do some business? That ship's casino lark, I could be on to something there. What's the score as regards getting paid?'

'Tell me what you've got – you were on that job in my time so –'

I leaned across her desk and tapped her blotter.

'Dot, sometimes I don't seem to be too clever but you ever know me pull a stroke on you? Isn't this town full enough of chiselling bastards without you and me playing silly girls with each other? Come on, we were friends once –'

'Friends?' she snorted. 'Did we ever behave like friends? Go to each other's houses? Lend each other cups of sugar? Go on holiday together? What the hell –'

'In this town if we've known each other longer than a year that's friendship. Let's not get sloppy. I've seen that geezer Coddington. Also the girl dealer. What's it worth if I sort them out and chuck 'em in your direction?'

'I was to get another six hundred if we wrapped the job up. I'd say three hundred to you would be fair.'

'Okay. I could wrap it up this week with luck.'

She sat back, small white hands clasped on her stomach.

'Finding it tough on your own, are you?' she said, not too sarcastically.

'I got an office in Mayfair. It's in the book under the name George Fitch. He's dead. By the way, who was young Mister Smooth?'

'Any of your business?'

I shrugged.

'I've seen him before, that's all.'

'His name's Paul Shirriff. He works for National Security Systems – he's a career object, a desk-wallah but ambitious. He wanted to be my partner. I told him I'd hire him at seventy a week.'

'I'll be your partner if you're looking for one.'

'He's got dough to invest and I told him to take a running.' She snorted. 'Twenty years it's taken me to build this outfit, you think I'm giving away bits of it to young smoothies?'

'I'm not a smoothie, am I?'

'No, you're all rough edges, you are. I bet you don't last three months running your own set-up.'

'You may be right. Three hundred, you said?'

'I wouldn't pay you anything, you bastard, if I had a choice.'

'So glad we're friends again.'

I went back to Shepherd Market, I got a meter in Curzon Street and walked under the arch to the pedestrian court with the four phone kiosks in the middle. I was in a hurry to get to the carsi but I did notice the two young blokes on the corner, I remembered thinking they were a bit on the young side to be needing whores at that time in the afternoon, sober.

Two of Christine Bunn's secretary girls were coming out of her office as I reached the landing. Great racket, that, supplying temps to firms who won't pay good enough wages for full-time girls but are happy to fork out fifties and sixties a week for agency casuals.

I dived into the loo, unzipped and sat down. Phew. Nice loo, too. Clean towel on a rail by the hot-water geyser, a cake of pink soap in a little plastic dish on the basin, two rolls of blue, double-strength, soft-tissue by the cistern, a white mat on the lino floor and a tufted lavatory seat in eggshell blue. Plus a deodorant stick fixed to the inside of the lavatory pan.

I've been in worse living-rooms.

She must have seen me passing her door.

'Mister Hazell?' I heard her saying.

'In here,' I grunted.

When I zipped up and came out she was standing in her own door looking impatient.

'Two men came asking for you,' she said snappily. 'They said they'd be back later, they didn't give their names. I wish you'd ask your clients not to ring my bell when you aren't in, I'm extremely busy.'

'Yeah, all go, innit?' I said cheerily, pushing on up the stairs. The hell with her, snooty little bitch.

There was no mail for me. This was no shock because nobody knew my address. So who were the two men who'd asked for me by name? Westminster City Rates maybe.

Sitting behind my desk, looking brisk, I called Mr Barclay at R. K. Brown Cruises Ltd. His secretary wasn't going to put me through but I told her to tell him it was James Hazell about the SS *Apollo*. When he came on I said *actually* I'd wanted to get in touch with his boy Kevin for a drink next time Kevin was in London. I made it sound like Kevin and I were great pals. He said he'd give Kevin my message. Perhaps I could come down and spend a weekend at their Sussex place?

I said Kevin would have to ring me at my new number as I was no longer with Miss Wilmington. I was setting up on my own and doing very nicely. I didn't actually knock Dot but I said it was just possible, being a lone operator, I might turn up something new about that *Apollo* job.

Being Kevin's best friend, practically one of the family, it didn't require too many sledge-hammer questions to get him to tell me what Dot's deal had been.

For the services of an operative they'd been paying her forty a day and expenses. On the identification and apprehension of any person or persons proved to be embezzling casino funds, provided this resulted from the activities of her operative, she was to be paid a further sum of twelve hundred quid.

Six hundred she'd told me, the lying bitch. I had to laugh. Not so much a lie as a half-truth.

We looked forward to meeting again and rang off.

I lit an Embassy, opening a new pack and dropping the gift coupon into the drawer with the plastic Walther PPK. I had to put the spent match back in the box. That's what I could get with the gift coupons – an ashtray. I shut the drawer and reached for the phone.

It rang anyway.

'Could I speak to Mister James Hazell?' said a superior female voice.

'Who wants him?' I said.

'Hang on, I have a call for you,' she sang. For a moment I felt I was being watched.

'Paul Shirriff of National Security Systems here,' he said, sounding smooth enough to skate on. But I hadn't long come from sharing a cabin with Kevin Barclay and my listeners knew the difference between a real snob accent and the kind you pick up from the correspondence course.

'We met this afternoon in Miss Wilmington's office,' he said.

I took a deep breath. I still hadn't admitted I *was* James Hazell. What kind of bugging miracles were these bastards working?

'Oh yeah?' I grunted.

'I rang her a few minutes ago, she told me how to get in touch with you. I say, I wonder if you'd have time for a quick noggin with me tonight?'

'I don't drink –'

'What I had in mind was a general chat – you're in Mayfair, aren't you?'

'Where else?'

'I'll nip over your way – it's such a drag getting over here to our shop in the Elephant and Castle. Bar of the Connaught suit you – say about half-past six?'

'Well, what's it –'

'Fine. See you –'

'Hang about.'

'Yes?'

'Nothing – I just wondered if you'd be wearing your helmet so's I'll recognize you.'

'Will I be doing *what*?'

'Don't be late,' I said, 'you know what they say, Helmet by Moonlight.'

'I'll be seeing you at six-thirty then,' he said, sounding a bit puzzled. Either he had no sense of humour or he didn't like helmet jokes. National Security Systems was one of the big outfits that run private police forces to look after bank and payroll deliveries and keep empty office blocks safe from homeless squatters and other anti-social elements.

Of course they aren't legal policemen. Their skidlid helmets are white and their uniforms green and those big sticks are not offensive weapons but merely to rap the knuckles of shotgun desperadoes.

Every time I see one of their armoured cars outside a bank with three or four heavies in helmets stroking their big sticks, I think of my father's friend Dick Bridges. He was in that helmet brigade for a while. He was so tough he used to hide his eyes at the bloodthirsty bits in Tom and Jerry.

He gave it up in the end because he lost his stick and was too embarrassed to tell them.

I don't say they're all like that, of course.

You need a lot of guts to wear those helmets in public.

It was about ten to five when I heard the footsteps on the stairs. I was just going to ring Mrs Spencer and tell her she was all set for a misadventure verdict and a happy ending on Thursday. It was twenty to five on my watch, which meant it was ten to five. A lot keep their watches fast but I reckon that's only making the grave come quicker. Life seems longer, somehow, if you're always ten minutes in the past.

At first I thought the footsteps were more of Christine Bunn's temps. What I couldn't understand was why the old days had gone when people were either bosses or workers. Now the big trend was to agencies. Everybody seemed happy yet where was the money actually coming from that was making millionaires out of the big agents?

The feet came on up. Somebody knocked on the door of the back room, the one which still had Fitch's sign up. I opened the door of the front room, the one with the Private sign. There were two of them, the youngish blokes I'd seen down below on the corner. One was bigger than the other but neither was a bantam.

'We've to see Mr Hazell,' said the big one.

'He's nipped out,' I said, 'can I give him a message?'

'Nah, we'll hang about an' wait if he ain't gonna be too long. Down the boozer is he?'

'They're not open yet. Wait in my office if you like.'

'Ta. Could do wiv a warm, bit Naughton outside.'

They sat down on my easy chairs and watched me without embarrassment. I sat behind the desk.

'Yeah, he's needing clients,' I said conversationally, nodding at the partition.

'You in wiv him are yer?' asked the small one. He was wearing a zipper jacket without a collar and a clean flannel shirt in a small check. Like his pal his hair was short and pressed flat on his skull. The big one was wearing a white shorties raincoat which wasn't buttoned but which he was holding together by his hands in the pockets.

'Just neighbours,' I said. Then I snapped my fingers. 'Shit!'

'Wot's up, squire?' said the big one.

'I clean forgot – are you Mister Copeland? I was to tell you he'd be back at five.' Then I frowned. 'How did you get in, by the way, that speaking lock gadget's a dead loss.'

'There was these two chicks comin' out,' said the smaller one. I caught his quick look at his pal. His eyes flicked back at the partition door.

'Is one of you Mr Copeland?' I said, scratching my jaw and pretending to be looking for something on the desk.

'Nah, we've brought a message from Mr Copeland,' said the bigger one. He nodded back at the partition door. His eyes didn't leave my face. 'That's handy.' His eyes smiled.

'Yeah,' I said, reaching down to the bottom drawer. I had a pretty shrewd suspicion what they'd come to do. I should have guessed that nothing would ever be simple dealing with Copeland.

I got Tel's model gun in my hand. It felt too light to be convincing but it was worth a try.

'So wot's your name then?' asked the smaller one. He was about twenty-two, very fresh in the complexion, clear brown eyes. Likeable, you'd think.

'Me?' I said, raising my eyebrows.

There was no point in putting it off any longer, for they were obviously here to stay. 'I cannot tell a lie,' I said, shrugging, 'I'm James Hazell. What was the message from Copeland?'

They looked at each other and exchanged little smiling nods.

'Thought you was, actually,' said the big one. 'I'm Colin and he's Mel.' He bent his head and started to lift his reggie out of the seat. I brought up the gun and put my elbows on the desk, holding it in front of me.

He sank back into the chair.

'Colin – Mel,' I said, nodding at each in turn. 'You the frighteners, are you?'

'Wot's that you got there then?' said Mel, looking at the gun. 'You got a licence for a shooter?'

'Yeah, people are always trying to lean on me, funny, innit?' I held the gun up and pretended to be examining it for the first time. 'You two remember a villain from up Islington way – Keith O'Rourke?'

'Nah, we don't know no villains, do we, Mel?'

'Remember he got put an end to in a house in Putney? About a year ago. Bloke got away with it – self-defence.'

'Oh yeah, could be I read about it in the linens.'

'Me that did it,' I said, shaking my head as if puzzled. 'So what's the message then?'

Their eyes kept moving from the gun to my face and back again. You could hear thinking wheels working out the odds. Was I for real with this thing? Was Copeland worth getting shot for? I closed my left eye and aimed the shooter at the wall.

'Just give me the message and then piss off,' I said, pleasantly.

'You was botherin' Uncle Sidney,' said Colin. 'He wants you to leave him alone, dunnee? You could git hurt botherin' Uncle Sidney.'

'Uncle Sidney Copeland? And you're Colin and Mel. Hey – why don't you say it the other way then you could be Mel and Colly. Uncle Sidney's melancholy nephews.' I grinned that way where you show all your teeth. 'Well, you tell Uncle Sidney that if he don't show here tomorrow morning he's down for a most awful shock. Right? Now, scarper, Mel and Colly.'

They got up. I just sat there, letting my index finger touch the plastic trigger.

'You really the ice-cream wot shot O'Rourke?' asked Mel. He made as if to take a step towards the desk. I raised the gun slowly and pointed it as his stomach.

'Yeah, I've felt bad about it ever since. Mind you, he came after me with a pheasant gun.'

'We'd better tell Uncle Sidney that Mr Hazell is a dodgy bloke to be crossin',' Colin said calmly to Mel.

'Cheers,' I said, still not getting up. 'By the way I'll be watching out the window to make sure you don't forget to leave the building.'

They left, shutting the door politely behind them, Colin still holding the raincoat together with his hands in the pockets. I got up quickly and slipped into the back room. Their footsteps went down the stairs. I made sure the door was locked and then stood at the window, squinting down to see the pavement. They turned right and headed off.

I put in the next few minutes breaking the Post Office's code of secrecy to get hold of the number for London directory enquiries. I didn't have any telephone books but that wouldn't have made any difference – they've stopped printing the directory number in the phone books.

How's that for consumer relations – keeping their own numbers a secret in case people bother them with enquiries?

For London, I eventually discovered, you dial one-four-two. Don't tell the Russians.

When I did get through the girl told me that the subscriber at that address in Overlea Road was a Mrs Vera Copeland. She gave me the number. I dialled it, wondering if Copeland put the phone under his wife's name to dodge the bill or to let everybody know she was the boss.

A woman answered the phone. The Enemy!

'I'd like to speak to Mr Copeland,' I said.

'He isn't in,' she said. She sounded breathless. 'Who is it?'

'James Hazell.'

A hand went over the mouthpiece. Then he came on. He sounded cheeky even on the phone.

'Yeah?' he said.

'Uncle Sidney?' I said. 'Hazell here. You own a couple of comics called Mel and Colin? Your melancholy babies are they?'

'Oh, you,' he said. 'You sound very jolly.'

'You broke your promise, Uncle Sidney, you sent those two instead of coming yourself. I've told them to tell you to make sure you get along here tomorrow. All right? And never mind your grafting – I want you here in the morning, right?'

107

'What did these geezers say?' he asked, sounding just a bit worried.

'Once I showed them my water-pistol they didn't say a lot, actually.'

'I don't know nuffin about any of that. My friend couldn't make it today. I dunno about tomorrow.'

'I'll give you till twelve then I'm going to have a chat with Vera. Okay?'

'Yeah, definite. Sorry about that.'

It was ten past six when I locked up and set off to meet Paul Shirriff in the Connaught. The light was going and the wind had turned cold enough to drive people off the streets. There's always a lull at that time in Shepherd Market, the interval between the straight daytime citizens going home and the horny punters arriving for the evening cash and bash trade.

I turned left into the forecourt that leads under the arch to Curzon Street. I'd just passed the phone boxes and was level with Cheevers the hairdressers when I heard those unmistakable gravelpit tones.

'I'll give you Mel and Colly, you berk,' said the big one, stepping out of a doorway in front of me.

He moved very easily for such a big bloke. I stood still. Then I got hit, hard and solid into the backs of my knees. In a flash I crumpled to the ground.

Chapter Eleven

I started to twist to one side so that lightning couldn't strike twice in the same place. But I couldn't get up. I was shoved down on my back, staring up at Mel.

Colly's face joined Mel's. He took one hand out of his pocket and let the raincoat fall open.

He'd been holding it that way to hide the pick-handle. They both stared down at me. Funnily enough, the pick-handle made me feel better. Two real heavies wouldn't have needed it. I was in no great pain, just feeling a bit silly.

'Only we had this message to deliver,' said Colly, 'we'd like it if your man Hazell would make himself scarce round Uncle Sidney. Got it?'

He bent down. The explosion erupted in my ear. I could see Colly's face mouthing something at me but I couldn't make any sense of it. Mel had sunk his boot into my skull. Colly's face was grinning. I saw him taking a double-handed grip on shiny wood.

I twisted round and snatched at one of Mel's size nines and yanked his foot so hard he went over.

Colly had a swing at me with the pick-handle but I was already coming up in a crouch and the middle of the stick bounced against my shoulder. I pushed him in the chest and stepped back, giving Mel a swift kick into the jaw beneath his ear. It felt like a good un, a solid, meaty thud.

Colly came at me with the pick-handle raised above his right shoulder. I backed quickly until I found myself against the phone box.

He swung at my head. I ducked. Wood crashed against iron. I thumped my fist into his throat. He fell backwards, slowly, choking, his hands at his neck, the pick-handle clattering on the pavement.

Mel was getting up slowly. I picked up the pick-handle and gave him a serious whack on the ribs. To tell the truth the pick-handle seemed such a lethal weapon once it was in my hands, balancing nicely, that I only aimed it at him half-strength. It was enough.

They lay close together, groaning. I threw the wooden chap between them. By now I could sense faces watching us from the buildings.

'Tell Uncle Sydney I'll see him tomorrow,' I said. My ears were still ringing. 'If I wasn't in a hurry I'd bring you some blankets,' I said, walking off through the darkened arch.

The sensible thing would have been to hurt those two so seriously they'd never want to tangle again. Nobody would have blamed me for breaking their legs and arms. I didn't because of Keith O'Rourke, the bloke I'd shot through the head.

Soon as that pick-handle was balanced smoothly in my hands I'd felt the same lurking thrill coming to the surface. Kill the bastards. Just how I'd felt when O'Rourke came up the stairs with a shotgun and I'd had a pistol in my hand and was waiting for him, all the odds in my favour.

Nobody had blamed me for shooting O'Rourke. It was self-defence, cut and dried.

I was the only one who knew I'd *enjoyed* it.

It looks very jolly when it's pesky redskins being shot off horses by John Wayne but I'd found out. Killing people for real is nasty. It leaves a stain. You tell yourself it was him or you but all the time you're thinking that *he* could still be living and enjoying a laugh and watching his kids grow up.

As I walked across Curzon Street on my way to the Connaught Hotel in Carlos Place I tried to tell myself I was improving but deep down, at least an inch, I knew how near I'd been to crippling those two lads.

Shirriff was at a table in the suave bar. He looked at home.

His face was so smooth he had to be an evening shaver. His cream shirt had not a crease or a mark on it. His hands were clean and his nails manicured.

I kept my hands in my coat pockets and felt like a layabout.

'Sorry I'm late,' I said, 'two blokes jumped me in the Market.'

'I thought muggers only picked on old ladies,' he said, flashing a two-second smile at me. 'What's yours?'

The waiter's tray was at my ear before I'd thought. I stared at Shirriff's smoothie face. It seemed to have a built-in sneer. We were about the same age.

I could just imagine his eyebrows going up when I asked for an orange juice.

The hell with it. I was fed up sounding like a medical case.

'Large brandy,' I said.

'And another glass of dry white wine for me,' he said. He gave me a cool look. 'You a hard drinker or is it just to steady your nerves?'

'I haven't had a drink for two years,' I snapped.

He didn't blush or say sorry or even lower his eyes. He just kept looking at me. His eyes were a light greeny-grey. Aggressive eyes.

'Why did they jump you?' he asked.

'Putting in the frighteners it's called,' I said. 'I was to be warned off.'

'And have you been – warned off?'

I shrugged. The waiter brought over the drinks. Shirriff dropped a pound note on the tray. The waiter lifted a corner of the white napkin but Shirriff was too bigtime for change. I picked up the brandy glass. After all that time the fumes seemed very strong.

I had a sniff but put down the glass without tasting it.

'So what's your angle then?' I said, delving for my fags and telling myself to simmer down.

He picked up my packet of Embassy. 'Smoke these for the gift coupons, do you?'

'Take one if you want,' I said. He shook his head disdainfully. I took the cigarette from my mouth and noticed that

111

my hand was trembling. He saw it too. He raised an eyebrow.

'Funny that,' I said, 'two blokes only came at me with a pick-handle – you'd think I'd have been shaking while it was happening instead of afterwards.'

'I phoned the Wilmington woman when I got back to my office,' he said, ignoring my heroic modesty. 'She says you're a good operator but not too bright. She doesn't seem to think you'll make it on your own. Tell me – how do you see your future?'

'Never think about it, do I?'

He smiled patronizingly. London was crawling with plastic smoothies like him, career hounds, self-taught pricks who'd left their council houses and gorblimey dads so far behind you couldn't see 'em with spy-glasses.

I picked up the brandy glass and had my first taste in all that time.

It tasted just like brandy.

The ceiling didn't fall in and my face didn't blow up, as far as I could tell.

Best of all – I didn't immediately want to shout for the bottle. I let out a big sigh and gave him a sight of my teeth.

'So what's your problem, squire?' I said cheerily.

He bridled at that. Like all these artificial career-bashers he only heard you when you said something that could be taken as a dig.

'Let's talk about your problem,' he said quickly. 'You're setting up on your own with an office in Mayfair? Private detective – one-man outfit?' He shook his head. 'All a bit tatty, isn't it?'

'True.'

'In my case I'm bored. I can't get any higher at National Security Systems. I'm in the process of putting out feelers in various directions –'

'Keep away from the Boy Scout hut then.'

'– I'd like the challenge of something new. I know the security business inside out – I started out to be a solicitor so I'm well versed in the law.' He raised his hands as if I was a full

112

Albert Hall. 'I'm bored – life has become so damnably pre-dictable, do you know what I mean?'

'Yeah,' I said seriously, 'like this mate of mine, he's only gone to live in South Africa, hunnee? So he says to the bloke, what d'you do for sex out here in the veldt – and the bloke says – ostriches, man. So he gets out there and sees this ostrich and rams it in. So the ostrich lifts its head out of the sand and takes off at sixty miles an hour. It's about sunset when he comes limping back to the farm. What happened says his mate. Well, he says, through his bruises and cuts, it was ecstasy for the first fifteen miles – then I got out of step.'

Shirriff stared at me with a heavy frown. I gave him a wink and had another sip. He blinked and carried on as if I hadn't spoken.

'Security consultancy is one possibility – you buy your in-surance through a broker who gives you independent advice – why not the same kind of service for security? Everything from locks to staff vetting. Yes?'

'Good idea,' I said enthusiastically, 'I break into factories and you come along in the morning and sell them new locks?'

'Not just factories – country houses, offices, museums, churches, private art collections –'

'Could be a good earner, I expect. Not my kind of racket though.'

'Oh – what kind of racket are you in then? Does it pay well? Is there a future in it? Are you going to spend the rest of your life fending off pick-handles?'

'Have I got a budgerigar? Do I ride a bike? What is this – twenty bleeding questions?'

Shirriff was long finished with listening.

'You see,' he said, jabbing his index finger at me like a kid pretending he's shooting Indians, 'I'm a top-class organizer – full of ideas. I won't insult you by coming on with the fake modesty bit – I know I'm good. What I need is a counter-balance, somebody who'll complement my abilities.' He looked at me deeply. 'Get my drift?'

'Well –'

'Tell me, what kind of work are you getting?'

'This and that, not –'

'Administration, business-sense, somebody to direct and channel your output – that's what you need. Tell me specifically what cases you're on now.'

'This and that.'

'I'm talking about the possibility of a partnership,' he said coldly, 'I think you can assume that I'm not out to steal your clients.'

'Get away,' I said. 'Listen, squire, first rule in this racket – be a loyal son to your mother.'

He frowned.

'What's your mother got to –'

'Learn to keep mum,' I said.

'Are you willing to consider and discuss this seriously?'

'Yeah,' I said, 'I'll consider it.' I looked at the ceiling. Then at him. 'Okay. I've decided against. Sorry about that.'

'I like people with a sense of humour,' he said, smiling. 'It's so –'

'Listen,' I snapped, 'I'm no Einstein but what I do I do all by myself, right? If I was going to have a partner I'd want a bloke who could help me out with the pick-handles, right? Blokes like you? Desk-bashers, office politics, too busy planning career jumps to do any actual work, bleeding Beau Brummels without any bottle –'

'I hardly think that –'

'I can see your game, mate, I go out and do the graft and you act brave with my money behind the office door? Where d'you come from?'

'Er – Leytonstone. Why?'

'Thought so. Took elocution, did you? Bet you don't like your old dad with his cloth cap embarrassing you in front of the posh neighbours.' He just sat there, his big eyes watching me, his face giving nothing away. 'You ask Dot if you can be her partner – she turns you down so you pick on me – and we've only just said hullo in her office? What you got – a few hundred quid? That's enough to buy a thick-ear like me, I suppose?

Yeah, well stuff your money and your partnership, mate, you're the sort of bloke I detest most of all.'

I made a grim face and got ready for ructions.

'I wish you'd think about it,' he said, standing up. He looked at his watch. 'Sorry I've got to dash – give me a buzz when you've pondered a bit. I think there's a lot we could do together. Bye.'

And off he went. He stopped at the bar and said something to the waiter, probably tipping him to remember his name next time, artificial bastard.

But no. He'd only paid for another large brandy, which the waiter brought over on a tray. So there I was, sitting in a posh bar in front of my second large brandy and nobody to talk to? Outflanked me, hadn't he?

The hell with pride, I polished off his brandy and left the Connaught and went to a couple of Mayfair pubs and ended up at this pricey discotheque in Bond Street, not that I dig discotheques but this one isn't so much for the music as the pulling.

You don't have to pull very hard, either. All the customers know why they're there. I spent a few quid on a few drinks for the lovely who elected herself Miss Right for the night and told her it would be a pleasure to drive her home.

To Ilford?

Gordon Bennett!

At the gate of this semi-detached house she announced that to be honest she was Mrs Right and what she usually did was get the bloke to drive round the corner and 'do it' where there was a dark bit to park the car.

I kicked her out and drove all the way back across London without seeing a single cop. Tell the truth I didn't remember seeing much of anything.

Chapter Twelve

When the front door bell went about eleven the next morning I was coping with the iron turban. There was a coating of rubber solution on my tongue. My guts were suffering something chronic. First taste of booze I'd had in near on two year and I had serious doubts if I'd make it to lunchtime.

'Copeland here,' said his voice from the box.

I pressed the buzzer to let them in. I heard their heavy crunches on the squeaky stairs. A hand rapped smartly on the glass part of the rear door. I opened the other one.

'Enter friends,' I said, trying to sound confident and cheerful.

Copeland alias Collins alias Coddington came in, followed by the big specimen with the pock-marks. Out in the street Big Blondie had only been conspicuous. In a room he was startling. He followed so close behind the little man he might have been on a lead. Every Irish joke invented could have been re-scripted with him in the starring role.

I got behind the desk just in case but they sat down. He grinned at me, the little man the two lads had called Uncle Sidney. His complexion was bright and ruddy, the kind that doesn't tan easily, which was handy for a bloke who went on secret sunshine cruises.

'We've received each other's messages then, old boy,' he said, with an air of confidence that wasn't too noticeable when I was making him sweat in his van a couple of days before. Maybe I'd have to slip in the magic word Battersea.

Twickenham I wasn't going to mention, not yet. That was my fifth ace.

'How's Mel and Colly?' I said. 'Bit naughty that, wasn't it?'

'Don't blame the lads, they got a bit riled you takin' the piss outa their names an' that. This is Desperate anyway.' He looked at the big fellow. 'You'll have to agree – that's a rascal of a suit he's got on.'

'A rascal of a suit?' I said. 'I like that, I might even use it.'

'It's yours, old boy,' said the little man, waving a neat little hand. 'Still, we ain't here to put up wiv Oscar for me witticistics.' He gave me a sad spaniel look. 'Sorry about that little family get-togevver I arranged.'

'No, you'd have to do better than that,' I said.

'Well you didn't expeck me to give in wivout a fight, did yer?' He winked. Then he looked at Desperate, whose big evil face was following the conversation tennis-style. 'Cor, Desp, that is a rascal of a whistle. It don't fit you anywhere, do it?'

'Shut up an' git on wiv the bisnis,' Desperate growled.

'Sorry about his coarse manner,' Copeland said to me, 'he was brought up rough in Acne Marshes, wurnt yer, Desp?' He looked at me. 'Acne Marshes – got it?'

'You rotten little berk,' said the big man, grinning.

'So you're our man,' I said, 'sorry, I can't go on calling you Desperate, can I?'

'It's Desmond Cooper, innit?' He craned forward to see if I was writing it down. 'Desmond Cooper.'

'I'll remember it,' I said, careful not to laugh. Copeland taking the mickey was one thing but from me it might deserve football with my stomach.

'I've told Desp – I mean, Desmond – you said you'd pay any fines involved an' thirty nicker on top,' said Copeland, 'only I've said you'll probably want to bung him anuvver score to make it up to the round half a hundred.' He gave me a fast wink with the eye farthest away from the big man.

Desmond Cooper smiled as if he'd pulled off the greatest coup since the Great Train job.

'He knows exactly what's expected, does he?' I asked.

'No problem. He'll have Sir Oliver sick wiv envy.'

He winked at me again. I couldn't believe he was for real, this bald little gorblimey joker who went on cruises and who was a snob house-owner in Twickenham and a pavement shark in the West End. With a wife called The Enemy up there in Stamford Hill. He gave me a smile.

'You must be quite a capable chap, old boy, seein' off the boys like that.'

'You overmatched them,' I said. He rubbed his hands together. God knows what part he thought he was playing – or what role he had me marked down for. I said I hoped we wouldn't be pulling any more strokes on each other.

'Nah, you're a force to be reckoned wiv, old boy, anybody sends Colin and Mel home wiv a thick ear gits my respect,' he said. He sounded as if he was taking the mickey but his face was all sincerity. 'An' once anyone gits my respeck they get no more aggravation from me. Ain't that right, Desp?'

'Git on wiv the fakkin bisnis,' growled Our Hero.

'I give you a score now and we go to see this commissioner for oaths and you sign a statement,' I said. 'You have to say you screwed this Spencer with the cards and he was chasing you and you shoved him to the ground in the tube but he still came after you. That proves he wasn't suicidal, maybe more homicidal. You have to turn up at the Westminster coroner's court on Thursday and say it all in public.'

'That's all right, innit?' Desperate said to Copeland, appealing for reassurance.

'Would I put you into anythin' iffey?' said Copeland, his bright eyes opening wide and then closing, with his eyebrows raised. I recognized a Stan Laurel fan. The more I saw of Copeland the more I marvelled. As we were all business mates now I held out the fags. Desperate leaned out for one. Copeland grimaced:

'Ain't you got the strenf of characker to give them things up?' he said. 'Killin' you, ain't they?' He looked disparagingly at Desperate. 'You'd be quicker eatin' them.'

I relaxed. I couldn't see why he'd want to sneak out of the deal now. We were all suited. Desperate was delighted to get half a hundred, Uncle Sidney was picking up a ton and a half and he was also under the mistaken belief I would be off his back. Mrs Spencer was getting the evidence she needed for a death by misadventure verdict. I was cleaning up a good case and earning well.

And once I had this one sewn up I was going to drop on Uncle Sidney like a concrete cloudburst.

Happy days for everybody.

Pity Mr Spencer couldn't be around to see how jolly his little accident had made everybody.

I made an appointment by phone and we took a cab over to a notary's office in the Strand. Desperate didn't so much make a statement as grunt answers to his prompters. Still, we weren't putting him up to tell a tale and I reckoned he could be trusted to remember the truth.

It was when the solicitor asked him how much they'd cheated Mr Spencer out of that Desperate became eloquent.

'We didn't have *nothin*' off ov him, did we?'

'I beg your pardon,' said the solicitor.

'We was just startin', wurnt we?' Desperate explained, shoving his finger at the lined foolscap as if he wanted each precious word to be recorded. 'He's bunged his oncer down an' we tell him to fakk off out ovvit, jacks the minimum, everybody knows that, doaney? But Bonnie the dog-eye give us the office that the Old Bill's loomin' so we're on our toes only he's said we owed him a nicker's winnin's – obvious the geezer's a dumbo. Stoopid berk, we don't ever let 'em bet for less than a jacks, do we?'

'Less than a what?' asked the solicitor.

'A jacks.'

'A jacks?'

'Like a flim.'

'A flim?'

Desperate looked at the ceiling in exasperation. Then, with some patience, he held up his right hand with five fingers showing.

'A handful,' he said.

'Oh – five pounds?'

Desperate blew with relief.

'Yeah,' he said reluctantly, 'if that's wot you wanna call it.'

'He's a rascal wiv the colourful dialogue, old Desmond,' said Copeland, winking at the solicitor and me.

'And has he a barrow in the market place?' quipped the lawyer. Desperate frowned at him.

'Wot's he on about?' he demanded, 'I ain't got no fakkin barra, have I, it's you its got the barra down Leyden Street, innit, Sid?'

So Copeland had *another* iron in the fire – a stall in Petticoat Lane.

'Never mind all that, we ain't got all day,' he said, just a little bit irritated. 'Anyway, it's Colin and Mel works the barrer.'

The lawyer led Desperate through the rest of his statement. I stood at the window, smoking and watching Copeland. Of course Petticoat Lane only operates one day a week, for a man of his energy probably just light relief to earn him a few bob on a Sunday.

With all the irons he had in it that was no ordinary fire, more like London's burning fetch water.

It took them half an hour to type up Desperate's statement and for him to sign copies of the deposition and for a clerk to witness his signature and the seal to be put on them.

Desperate was given one copy, the notary kept another and I came away with the other four in a big brown envelope. It was about half-past one when we came out into the sunshine of the Strand.

I handed Desperate four fivers.

'The rest you get at the coroner's court on Thursday morning,' I said.

'Easier than geein' up mugs wiv the boards, innit?' said Copeland, patting the big fella's back. He gave me a quick look. 'Mister Hazell's bungin' me a score for arrangin' all this, ain't yer, Mister Hazell?'

'No, Mrs Spencer is,' I said, watching a couple of girls go by on four-inch soles. Never been kinky about stiltwalkers, myself. Copeland frowned at me. 'If you want a down payment we'll have to go to my bank,' I said.

'Nah, I trusts yer, give us it Thursday,' he said. 'Course if there was any hitch I could send some better messingers than Colin and Mel next time I expeck.'

'Mutual trust makes the Stock Exchange tick,' I said.

'You got it, old boy. Come on, let's git up the Wardorf for a taste, celebrate our big deal an' that. Yer welcome to make one wiv us, Mister Hazell.'

I licked my dry lips with my coated tongue.

'Why not?' I said. 'I can phone the good news to the client from up there.'

As we waved at taxis from the kerb I told myself I was definitely not going back on the grog, only tagging along to keep Copeland in sight. Mrs Spencer's problem was taken care of. From here on I was chasing a slice of R. K. Brown's twelve hundred quid.

It was only a five-minute taxi trip, round Trafalgar Square, up Lower Regent Street, round Piccadilly Circus, up Shaftes-bury Avenue to Cambridge Circus and then into Charing Cross Road. Copeland and I sat on the proper seats, Desperate's big pock-marked face facing us from a fold-down.

Copeland kept up a cheery conversation the whole way, a lot of it jokes at Desperate. He just stared out at the people on the sunny pavements. I was careful not to join in the piss-taking. Copeland handled the big menace like a bear on a chain but I'd seen him hulking over the three-card victims and I knew better than delude myself he was safe.

We got out halfway up Charing Cross Road Uncle Sidney nominated Desperate to pay off the cab. He nodded for me to step back from the kerb and muttered:

'I don't git a hundred and fifty nicker off you he don't show at any court, know that, donchyer?'

'Look,' I said, holding my hands open, 'you know my office, you know all about me – you think I'd risk any clever stuff for the sake of a ton and a half? My business depends on every-thing turning out smooth.'

'Only I'm a ruthless sort of a joker beneath the jovial exterior,' he said, giving me a serious wink.

It was some years since I'd been in the famous Wardorf, just behind Charing Cross Road. I say famous, but not like coachloads of tourists taking snaps of the tatty entrance. Famous in fraternity circles.

You go up two flights of stairs and through a landing door and you're greeted by a suavo in a grey chalk-stripe, open-necked white shirt and Paisley cravat. He's The Colonel. He generally stands behind his small desk trying to look as if he's expecting The Duke at any moment and as if there isn't a length of lead-pipe on the ledge beside him.

Copeland put a scribble on the large book lying open on the desk and handed me the ballpoint – which was chained, to give you some idea of the tone – to sign whatever name I cared to bung down under the heading of *Guests*.

I slithered down a curvy line that nobody could prove was not J. Hazell.

'How's the wife and family then, Sid?' said the Colonel.

'Better'n nuffin.'

I followed him and Desperate into the smoky afternoon of the Wardorf.

It was a bigger room than most clubs, with windows at both ends. There were sixty or so men about town present – from the noise it could have been hundreds. Sunshine was coming in the rear windows above the pinball machines and bandits but nobody was letting daylight cast a gloom on the proceedings.

Small packs of men were watching the roulette wheel or the flashing lights among the pinball palm trees. Other men were slapping their trouser seats as the two o'clock from Cheltenham came up in full colour on the set at the far end of the long bar.

Not what you'd call a trendy lot, the Wardorf punters, more your unpressed suits and shirts and ties and an occasional set of sideburns from way back. Copeland led us to a space at the bar among all the geezers with no athletic or sporting interests. I recognized the bloke he went up to, the dog-eye who looked a bit like Robert Mitchum.

'What'll yer have, Sid?' he asked.

'A larger,' said Copeland.

'A lager yer mean?'

'Nah, a larger – I wanna larger one than you're usually buyin'. Scotch, yah berk.' He nodded for me to join in. 'Have you met? Jim – this is Bungalow.' The stout fella in the brown suit pumped my arm vigorously, as if he'd been dying to meet me all his life. Copeland said, 'Know why he's called Bungalow? Cos he's got nuffin upstairs, has he?'

'Wot're you havin', Jim?' asked Bungalow, fat fingers sliding a fiver out of his hip-pocket.

'Lager,' I said. Bungalow raised a finger and an eyebrow. Just like Mitchum. One of the two barmaids came to serve him. Tell the truth she was a bit like Mitchum as well, about the stomach anyway. I glanced round the room. I'd seen a lot of these faces in the past. Front and side profile faces. I won't say they were all villains in there but I did feel a bit like the parachutist who came down in the Dartmoor exercise yard and did ten years before anybody would believe him.

They were the cagey faces you see outside stadiums touting black market tickets from the side of the mouth. Their shoulders played as big a part in their chat as their lips and their eyes continually scanned the bar horizons for any sign of bother or free money.

Neat scotch was the general drink and nobody was checking calory charts. The square nation outside was in its usual state of crisis but in here the jolly band of conspirators was having a gargle and a giggle and giving not a monkey's for laws, taxes, morals or any of the rest of that old government moody.

With these blokes security was a few readies in the bin for today's booze-up and ambitions got no more grandiose than a preference for staying out of the nick. But if tomorrow brought a three-year lagging or a year's stretch or a three-month carpeting – well, it was all in the game, wasn't it?

Naturally they thought they were superior to the mugs who did straight toil but they spent half their stupid lives bunked up three to a cell wondering who was charvering the missus and aching for the sight of a red London bus.

No, I wouldn't get too sentimental about the bastards.

But – look at it this way. If the rest of us had any brains there wouldn't be scope for villains, would there? Not for the three-card merchants anyway . . .

'You don't mind me callin' you Jim, do yer?' Copeland said suddenly, 'only we might as well be friendly about it.'

'I don't mind, Uncle Sidney.'

He laughed.

Bungalow handed me the glass of lager. The first cold dollop washed away the taste of last night's brandy. I wasn't drinking so much as de-coking.

'How's the wife?' Bungalow asked Copeland, handing him his scotch.

'Compared with who?' Copeland retorted.

'He's a boy, innee?' Desperate said to me. 'Got an answer for everythin' he has.'

'A rascal, eh?' I said.

'That's it,' said Desperate, laughing and nodding and coughing all at once, 'a right little rascal.'

'Rascal?' chirruped Copeland. He did tend to squeak when he got emotional. 'It's because ov men like me that Europe's free today, innit?'

'You?' sneered Bungalow. 'You niver went near the fakkin kate in the war, yah berk.'

'Course I didn't! Me in the bleedin' army? Cor. Nah, I ignored the whole affair, din I?'

'So wot's Europe gotta thank you for then?'

'Stayin' out ovvit. If blokes like me had turned up for the bleedin' army we'd've lost. So I did me bit livin' two doors away under anuvver name, din I?' He frowned, looking closely at Bungalow, then at Desperate. 'Ugly sods, ain't they, Jim? Cor, just lookin' at 'em makes me believe more in birth control. I'll be back in a jiff.'

He was a big attraction in the Wardorf. He kept leaving us to give blessings to various people. Wherever he went he left them keeling over at his patter. A non-stop cabaret turn, that was Uncle Sidney the three-card shyster. Out there on the pavements he could screw the last pound note out of you and reduce grown men to tears but in here he was The Joker, the man who made 'em all laugh.

I'm not saying he was a great wit. Cheeky was more like it. A very fast eye for a weak spot and always careful to keep his insulting patter on this side of resentment.

Most of these merchants knew the art of staying alive on a penny, all very cute in their own way, but he was more, even if you didn't know about his double life and his flash house in Twickenham and his wig and his fancy girlfriend. He was more tuned-in, quicker – yet at the same time detached, never laughing so much at his own spiel that his eyes stopped darting round the room, the same lightning eyes that scanned the mugs' faces while his little red hands shuffled the cards.

Funny little hands they were. Clean nails and no hair – and red as if they were always cold.

I was looking forward to the moment when I told him I knew all about his secret life.

We'd see if he could make a merry jest then.

He came back to join us. I shouted up three more scotches and a lager. Four men came through the door and moved against the bar with smiles and nods.

Copeland's little hands were waving about as he told us some new Irish joke but I kept watching these new arrivals, one of them in particular.

Copeland looked round to see what was interesting me. A big smile broke over his fresh little face. Then he put his fingers to his mouth, as if he'd said something rude.

'Who is that geezer?' I asked, being careful, of course, not to point.

This bloke had caught my attention because unlike everybody else in there he was not laughing, telling a joke, rabbiting like a demon or waving his arms about.

He was about five foot eight, light brown hair cut short and combed flat; he had on a white shirt with a stiff collar and a dark tie with a small knot, a dark blue suit with wide shoulders and narrow trousers; he was also wearing a gold watch, a gold tie-clip and a gold ring. Apart from occasional sips at his glass he hardly moved. His face listened to what his three mates had to say but his eyes patrolled the room.

'It's Bunter, innit?' said Copeland.

'Bunter Begg by any chance?'

'That's him, Billy Bunter Begg,' said Desperate with more than a trace of respect.

'From Walthamstow, isn't he?'

'From everywhere more like it,' said Copeland seriously. 'Mister Big, innee? Top man. Oh yeah, if it happens in this town an' Mister Big Begg don't hear about it . . .' His eyebrows met in a frown and he shook his head as if warning me. 'He's not a casual sort so don't be larkin' about with him.' Then he laughed.

'I hear something about a reward of some kind?' I said. Desperate lowered his big head.

'He lost a big bundle not far back, just took a stroll it did, nobody knows how.'

'He's put it about there's five grand for the one wot tells him who had it away,' murmured Bungalow. We were all being careful not to let our eyes be caught looking at Begg.

'Yeah, five grand,' said Desperate, 'cor – I wish I noo somethin' –'

'You'd shop 'em, would yer?' said Copeland.

'For five grand? I'd grass on me Mum for five grand! You gotta be jokin', Sid – *five grand?*'

'Grass on yer mates for five grand would yer?' asked Copeland.

Desperate frowned as he recognized the moral dilemma.

'Well, maybe not me *mates* –'

Copeland snorted.

'It's because of men like you that Europe become a mess inna first place, innit?'

Desperate laughed and so did Bungalow but I didn't think Uncle Sidney was joking that time.

I was calling Mrs Spencer from the public phone on the landing beside the Colonel's desk when Bunter Begg the gangster came out to the lavatory.

'All right?' he said to the Colonel as he passed, giving me a quick up and down with light-coloured eyes that were as remote and distant as any I've known. It crossed my mind that the Wardorf might be one of the businesses he 'protected'.

'Hello,' said Mrs Spencer's voice.

'It's me,' I said, not particularly wanting the Colonel to hear any vital details. 'It's all wrapped up, everything's been signed, I thought I'd nip over to your place this afternoon with the hoojahs and we can settle –'

'No, I'd rather come into town and meet you,' she said quickly. 'I've got to see my bank head office tomorrow anyway – could I come to your office in the morning?'

'Okay, I'll be in by half-past nine.'

As I was putting the phone down Begg passed through into the bar. I was a couple of steps behind him. He let the door swing back in my face, although he couldn't have missed me so close behind.

I had three small lagers with Copeland and his mates from the three-card team and then I pushed off. They looked set for a long session. I arranged to meet them outside the Westminster Coroner's Court in Horseferry Road on Thursday morning.

We all shook hands. Begg gave me a blank eye as I passed his group. Then the door closed, the Colonel said farewell and it was back out into the real world where the honest worried people crowded the pavements and money was stuff they didn't pay you enough of for that sick joke called work.

I got a cab to Shepherd Market. The Stag had two tickets under the wiper. I left them as insurance against more tickets. If I was towed away I was just about fed up enough of tickets to let them keep the bleeding car.

There was no mail. I opened a window and got my feet up on the desk and lit a cigarette, despite Uncle Sidney's warnings.

I covered all possibilities and it still came back to ships' casinos. The computer had spotted a drop in the *Apollo* take but what had it missed? R. K. Brown ran five boats, each casino coining in good money. All cash, no receipts, no stock to check afterwards. Maybe the fiddle had been going on for years. Maybe the new computer had no kosher figures to check against.

The directors thought they had a foolproof system. Everybody does, till the thieves strike. When that gang was rooted out of the London airport car-park it was realized they'd been stealing three grand *a week*.

It's easy enough done, in a car-park or a casino. You infiltrate one bloke, he corrupts one of the straight staff, soon they're all at it, either too greedy or too scared to stop.

Those casinos had to be the source of Uncle Sidney's loot. The point was – did he belong to somebody else's set-up or was he the brains?

I had to find out if he'd ever been associated with any better-class villains than Desperate and Bungalow. When I handed this lot over to R. K. Brown Ltd I wanted to give them the whole shooting-match.

Poor Uncle Sidney, I thought, picking up the phone, you're going to regret the day you diddled Mr Spencer out of one lousy pound note.

I dialled two-three-oh one-two-one-two and asked the New Scotland Yard exchange for Detective Inspector Minty, Flying Squad.

In this racket you can't be too choosy.

Chapter Thirteen

Nobody trusts a copper.

When I was a kid in the East End I must have been the only boy in any of the streets we lived in who actually fancied policemen.

None of my family, not to mention everybody else, would have suffered emotionally if all the cops in London had gone over a cliff in a burning bus but I thought they were really something, especially detectives.

When I astounded my family by joining the Metropolitan my Mum and Dad still talked to me, which just shows you about parental love, but in some other houses my name was banned.

It took me five years to get into the Flying Squad and five minutes of having my ankle massaged by a car door to get out of the force again. Maybe the busted ankle was only an excuse.

The only people we seemed to have anything in common with were the very layabouts and villains we were supposed to be waging this relentless war on.

I was glad to get out of it. Like getting back on speaking terms with the human race.

Choc Minty was a good example of why nobody trusts a copper.

He was the bastard who'd find the dodgy angle in a Sunday School picnic. He'd had it on good authority that everybody in the world was crooked and the more of us he could get in clink the better he felt.

He was a big, red-faced Aberdonian. Diabolical is a good word to use for him while the dictionary authors try to invent something stronger.

Good cop, though. Honest? Try to bung him a few quid for an accommodation and you could say ta ra to your teeth.

He hated me for some reason. When we were in the same section he had this bee in his bonnet that I was bent.

Phoning him for a favour came very hard.

Thinking up what I could give him in return was even harder.

'I wondered when you'd turn up again,' he said in his harsh Scots voice when he phoned back about half-past three.

'I'm wondering if you could do me a favour,' I said.

'Were you? Last time I did you a favour it didn't turn out so well.'

'You mean O'Rourke?'

'Never mind all that. I'm busy.'

'About this other thing – could we have a meet?'

'A favour? I only do favours for people who give us co-operation.'

'I might have something for you in return. Little bit of information you might find useful.'

'Really? There's a pub in Hammersmith I might drop into on the way home tonight about six. You remember that pub we were in that night – the lorryload of electric blankets?'

'Bit horrible that one, wasn't it?'

'Aye but nobody'll see me with a fly boy like you.'

'Charming. It's thanks to men like me that Europe's free today.'

'You drunk?'

'No. I'll see you there round six.'

Grunt.

The pub Minty chose was rough even by Hammersmith standards. Of course there's good parts and bad parts of Hammersmith. This pub was as bad as any going.

Minty was already at the slopping bar when I pushed through the dingy saloon door.

It wasn't rough meaning violent – just horrible. The paper was coming off the walls in damp patches and the decor was like an old railway waiting-room with one difference. The lighting. I've never been in such a brightly-lit boozer. It was glaring.

The staff was an Irish bloke about twenty-five. He had the beer gut of a much older man. It was straining against a grey vest that in its turn was trying to pop out where his shirt buttons were missing.

From his pained movements and sharp sighs and groans it was possible he was suffering the worst hangover since Pisa. He hadn't shaved that day, although that was hardly likely to upset the clientele.

Actually I feel sorry for the Irish who come over here to wear big letters on their backs. They generally leave the wife at home on holy soil and only see her at Xmas to father next year's crop. In between Xmases they doss down in cheap rooms and send the wife's money home by postal order and drink themselves silly to fill up the void.

Thumping each other and kicking Chinese waiters is about the height of their swinging lives. They don't seem to have much interest in the local women and they tend to stick to their own pubs. 'It's gone Irish,' you'll hear people say about a rub-a-dub that's been taken over by the big men with the pixie ears. It's not meant as a recommendation.

I say sorry but not enough to want ten of them home for a cooked meal.

With his big red face and short crop and heavy clothes Minty didn't look too conspicuous at the beer-puddled bar but in my black sweater and suede jacket I felt as out of place as a male mannequin.

The ones nearest us, for instance, were wearing muddy boots.

Never mind their boots, they hadn't even scraped their hands or faces.

Minty gave me the fish-eye welcome. I asked him what he was having. He said he would just have another drop of Bells, a large one.

I asked the suffering barman for half of draught lager for myself.

The five building-site micks next to us weren't saying much at that stage. Just deep grunts of 'surely, surely'.

'So what's this favour?' Minty demanded.

'There's a bloke I'm on to, I'd like to know his form, his previous, known associates, it's –'

'That's against the rules. Or has getting away with shooting O'Rourke given you the idea you're beyond rules?'

'I know it's against the rules. Only if I can get him sewn up I'll be throwing him your way. I've already got him for part of an embezzlement caper but I could get a whole ring of them.'

'It's still against the rules. What good would it do me, taking a risk to help you earn your bloody fee?'

I'd thought a lot about what I could chuck Minty in return for finding out about Copeland's history. It had to be something that sounded good. Just enough truth in it to keep me in the clear afterwards.

Begg seemed to be the only answer.

I don't like a grass but he shouldn't have let the door swing in my face, should he?

'Oh aye, Billy Bunter Begg,' said Minty non-committally. He polished off that whisky, the glass lost in his big fleshy fingers. The five micks were listening heads down to a dirty joke. When they laughed it was towards the ceiling. Minty pushed his empty glass across the wet bar. I was only halfway down my lager.

Minty waited. I'd bought the last round but another facet to Minty's charm was this allergy. He always came out in spots when he had to buy a drink.

Never had a spot in his life, of course.

I just sipped my lager and let his thirst get the better of him. Thirsty lot, coppers. He asked the barman for another large Bells. Faced by my relentless silence he made a grim face and then raided the moth farm for a pound note.

I said I'd struggle down another half of lager.

Silly really but a victory all the same.

'So what about Begg then?' he growled.

'He's offering five grand reward for news of some loot he's

lost. It took a stroll from his safe deposit box. You not heard anything about it?'

He grunted something that could have been yes or no. I took it to be no.

'I hear it was ninety grand,' I said. 'If it wasn't hot it certainly wasn't kosher, because he didn't report it was stolen. Ninety grand sounds like his life's savings to me.'

'What safe deposit was he using?'

'I'm not sure. It seems to have happened in November or thereabouts. I'm wondering if it had anything to do with that night guard who got done over by that masked team and dumped in Epping Forest – that was around November, wasn't it?'

'Aye, it was,' he said emphatically. 'That was Bullion Stores, Great Portland Street. The guard's name was Lonsdale Oliphant. I remembered it because Oliphant was my mother's maiden name in Aberdeenshire – and this one was as black as the ace of spades. They jumped him in Foley Street coming off night shift, they bundled him in a van and tried to terrorize him into taking them back into the strong-room.'

'Gave him a bit of a hurting, didn't they?'

'Nothing too drastic. Three broken ribs, fractured cheekbone, one broken arm? Bastards duffed him up with an iron bar. I hope he still thinks loyalty's a paying virtue – I hear he's stuck in a bedroom in Brixton too jittery ever to face the street again. But they didn't get into the safe deposits. How could Begg be involved?'

'I don't know, do I? It seems a bit coincidental though.'

Behind him one of the five building-site micks was trying to remember the verses of some sad ballad. The others looked ready to fall weeping in each other's arms.

'How sure are you about this reward he's offering then?' he asked, his voice minus a lot of the aggression.

'I've heard about it from two sources. I don't know what use it is to you but it could be a lead to something.'

'Aye, could be.' He finished that whisky. I bought him another without looking too eager.

'The bloke I'm interested in has nothing to do with that,' I said. 'Think you'll manage to look him up for me?'

'Give us his name and I'll see.'

'He's got several this little bastard. He could be Sidney Copeland or Collins or Simon Coddington. He's about fifty, lives in Stamford Hill. Smalltime con-man – his usual game's the three-card trick, works with a team in Oxford Street. I think he could be involved in a bigger caper but I don't know who with. It's any associates I'm really interested in.'

'I'll have a look.' He looked at me, shaking his head and curling his upper lip against his nose. 'Give you full credit, you're a tricky bugger, Hazell.'

'You still aggrieved about O'Rourke? If it's any consolation I regret that more than anything else I've ever done.'

He snorted. There was no point in trying to convince him. He would never take anything I said at face value. I shrugged. The five Irish labourers were flinging arms round each other and swearing eternal friendship. An old woman had a row with the barman about the price of a bottle of sweet stout.

Minty and I left the pub around the time the five sons of Erin were beginning to snarl at each other. We were through the door before it was jackets off.

'What does a bloke like you do with his nights then?' Minty asked on the pavement, just before we separated.

'I dunno. Usual things. What do you do?'

'Bright lights is it? Chasing little dollies in discotheques? Me? I go home and try to forget for a minute that I spend my life in murky waters. I'll give you a ring.'

He always sounded a bit bitter but this last seemed to be from the heart. Maybe he was beginning to ask himself what it was all about. It's the usual question men start asking themselves when forty looms.

I walked to the side street where I'd left the car. It was half-past eight. Too early for lights out. Too late for optimism.

I drove back to Ravenscourt Park, stopping at a take-away to pick up half a chicken and chips. After I'd scoffed this lot it was only half-past nine and there was nothing on the vision so

134

I decided what the hell and looked up Locke in the phone book.

A man's voice answered so I said wrong number and rang off. It must have been George, the husband who'd gone the wrong way. He sounded a bit leery. I watched a documentary about outer space. Scientists had discovered strong evidence of anti-matter. Seemingly there were black holes out there in nowhere. Big deal.

Is there life on earth, that's the real question.

Minty phoned the next morning while I was sitting across my desk from the scintillating Mrs Spencer. I'd given her the four copies of Desperate Desmond's signed statement to give to her solicitor.

'So it looks set for you to collect the ten grand,' I was saying when the phone rang. She didn't leap about to any great extent.

'This Copeland,' Minty began, with none of your hypocritical questions as to health and happiness, 'he sounds a right no-body. Still, I suppose in your line you can't be too fussy. Want to hear it?'

'Not too impressive, is it?'

'Sidney Copeland, let's see – oh aye, born Hackney, nineteen-twenty. Approved school for thieving, nothing much, nineteen-thirty-nine, charged with being in possession of a shot-gun, six months, nineteen-forty-one charged with failing to report for military service, he did a year for that, nineteen-forty-five charged with being a deserter, did a year for that, nineteen-forty-seven charged with theft of clothing coupons, did six months for that – then there's a gap – nineteen-sixty-seven charged with obstructing the pavement, fined twenty-five pounds, nineteen-sixty-eight charged with obstructing the police to wit acting as lookout; for illegal street-betting, twenty-five pound fine, nineteen-seventy charged with con-spiracy to defraud, found not guilty at Middlesex Sessions – and that's your lot. Sounds like a real master-mind.'

'That all?'

'Aye.'

'Who was he conspiring with, the fraud case?'

'Just a minute – oh aye, Desmond Cooper, Francis McEvoy, Terence Hopkins. Want the addresses?'

'No, that's the three-card team.'

'A miserable bunch of petty hooligans. People pay you well for this class of work, do they?'

'Yeah. Thanks anyway.'

'Never mind the thanks, what else can you dig up about Begg?'

'I hear anything I'll give you a buzz.'

'You'd better.'

I put down the phone. Mrs Spencer was holding up the copies of Desperate's statement.

'You take these round to your solicitor this morning,' I said. 'Tell him Cooper will be at the court half an hour early. Don't tell him about the money, just to be on the safe side.'

She frowned. She held up the statements.

'It really does seem unfair that I should have to pay this awful man so much money – just to make him tell the truth,' she said.

'I agree,' I said whole-heartedly. 'If only the world was full of decent people. However – if you don't bung him the two hundred tomorrow he'll simply have one of those inexplicable memory lapses.'

I sat back and tried not to let the irritation show. I would have liked to snarl at her that some old East End jeweller had been beaten to death only the day before by a couple of teara-ways. Their haul was about sixty quid. Who the hell did she think she was to be moaning?

I told myself that but for her I'd never have got back on the trail of Copeland.

Maybe I still looked annoyed.

'I'll go to my bank this morning and draw it out,' she said quickly, almost apologetically. 'I'm very grateful to you, of course, Mr Hazell, don't think I'm not, I –'

'That's okay. There's also three days outstanding on my account, I can do you out a bill for it now and –'

'Can I settle that tomorrow as well?' she said quickly, looking at her watch, 'I'm supposed to be at my solicitor's office at half-past ten.'

'Of course,' I said with a forced smile.

Amazing how much bogus politeness flies about when the corpse is still fresh, isn't it?

She said a brave little goodbye and went off down the squeaky stairs. I went down a few seconds later to use the shared carsi. Loo, I mean.

Christine Bunn's door was shut. I would have liked a chat with her, just to start mending fences but the only conversational gambit I could come up with didn't sound like the way to soften a lady's heart:

Who buys the toilet rolls?

I sat in one of the easy chairs and looked across the desk at the empty space where I should have been. The room looked very bare. I got out my cigarettes and then decided against lighting up because there was no ashtray.

That made me think of Uncle Sidney, who said smoking was a filthy habit. Not bad, was it, from a swindling little hound like him.

I got my heels up on the desk and started to rehearse what I'd say to him tomorrow, the moment that inquest was over.

The phone rang as I was thinking up different ways to drop the bombshell. I knew he would want me to do it with a bit of style.

It was a long-distance call for Mr George Fitch. The man's voice had a north country accent. I said I wasn't Mr Fitch but Mr Hazell and that I'd taken over Mr Fitch's office. Perhaps he took this to mean I'd taken over the actual business. He said he'd been given Fitch's name as a good London enquiry agent. I said Fitch was dead, could I help?

He was a very worried man, I don't think he was too bothered what my name was. His fifteen-year-old daughter had run away from home in Carlisle a week before. She was mad about pop music and Carnaby Street clothes and was probably hanging about teenage rock clubs. His wife was going out of her mind.

I said his best bet were the police and the Salvation Army. He said he'd been to the police and given them a description but they obviously got so many of these cases they regarded them as routine.

He didn't care what it would cost but he wanted her found. I said any private enquiry agent who took his money for that kind of job was a shark. I think I convinced him that the Salvation Army and the police were the experts. He was glad of the chance to talk about it and thanked me for my advice. It was a twenty-minute call.

It did just strike me that turning away business might not be the most useful skill I could develop.

I decided to make a list of everything I knew about Sidney Copeland. There wasn't a bit of clean paper in the place. I decided to go out and buy a desk diary, an ashtray and some good-class stationery. The phone rang again. It was Paul Shirriff. He wanted to know if I'd thought any more on his partnership idea. I said I didn't want a partner.

He said he'd give me a ring next time he was coming up my way, we could have a drink and a chat.

I felt tired.

When I woke up the phone was ringing again. This time it was a firm of solicitors in Gravesend. I told them Fitch was dead but that I had taken over his office and was in the same line but they said thank you no, we've been dealing with Mr Fitch for some years, we'll make other arrangements. I said – but they rang off.

I went out to buy stationery and an ashtray. The weather was a little warmer. It was the first time I'd ever bought office stationery. At those prices it would have been as cheap to write messages on pound notes.

I took a carton of tea back up with me. When I got in the phone was ringing. This time it was a secretarial agency wanting to know when Mr Fitch was going to settle his outstanding account. I told them he was dead. The head lady came on. I told *her* he was dead. She didn't want to hear all these irrelevant details, when could they expect settlement?

138

I said I knew nothing about the man or his business. Dead, I said, spelling it for her. She said she would consult her solicitor. I said a spiritualist medium might be a better bet but she had no sense of humour.

I sat at my ease and drank my tea and flicked ash on to my new china ashtray. It seemed a shame to get it dirty. That was something else I had to buy – a waste bucket.

The phone was ringing again. A woman asked if there was any news about Mr Morrison's stamp collection. I said Mr Fitch was dead and she rang off in a hurry.

I decided to swallow it as far as the news about Fitch's death was concerned. If I was good enough to rent his Mayfair office I was good enough to take over his clients.

Naturally the phone didn't ring again that afternoon.

I got bored sitting there, even if it was in Mayfair. I decided to ring somebody. The first name that came to mind was Stephanie Parmenter. I'd promised to buzz her back in London and she wasn't to know I didn't mean it at the time.

That's always been one of my main character flaws. If I'm not actually working I can't remember what I'm doing here. Maybe if I had a wife to make kitchen shelves for I might discover the rich pastures of what they're now calling leisure but not having a wife is another of my deficiencies.

Regular old flaw show, that's me.

A sexy female voice answered.

'Stephanie's not here this afternoon, this is Tarra,' she said. I remembered hearing a lot about Tarra. They shared this two-bedroom flat in Paddington, only Stephanie preferred to say Bayswater, Paddington sounding too much like whoresville.

Stephanie had been living with a fashion photographer for six years. Their bust-up brought on the nervous troubles that made her doctor advise the cruise.

Tarra was another actress. She'd suggested they share a flat, having just been divorced for the second time. She didn't get too many parts so she did a lot of modelling.

In a confidential moment Stephanie told me Tarra's modelling wasn't exactly haute couture stuff. Her second husband, the wholesale blouse tycoon, had given her the boot when she'd brought back a nice little dose of gonorrhoea to the nuptial couch.

I didn't mention I knew all this.

'I met her on the cruise,' I said, 'my name's James Hazell, just tell her I rang.'

'Oh yes,' she said mysteriously, 'I heard about you and Steph. Must have been all that gorgeous moonlight, was it?'

'Yeah. Anyway, just say I rang –'

'Is there a number she can call you at?'

'Not really.'

'Of course – you're always out at sea in the moonlight aren't you?'

'Not really.'

'She's rehearsing a television today in Fulham.'

'Oh yeah. When's it going out?'

'Oh not for ages I should think. That whole scene is too grotty. She's stuck all day in a dreary church hall off North End Road. Why don't you ring her there?'

'I could do I suppose. What's the place called?'

I did better than ring.

I wasn't doing much good sitting in an empty office waiting for a dead man's telephone calls, was I?

I drove over to North End Road and found the church hall. There was nobody on the door so I just wandered in. They were out in the middle of the floor, walking about on chalk lines and muttering dialogue.

I leaned back against the wall and listened to how the magic gets on our screens. They were pretending to be in a hotel suite. Stephanie was wearing blue slacks, chunky sweater and cute little beret. The guy in charge was one of those virile forty-year-olds. He had a high-faluting accent but just to let everybody know the real situation he was wearing the latest in Maoist denims and shouting *fuck* a lot.

The male star was a guy I'd seen on the vision a hundred

times, a kind of cut-price Michael Caine with an impressive pair of hairy arms. He was wearing pale blue slacks and a sleeveless Fair Isle sweater with a low neck, plenty of hair on his chest.

The brutal image was spoiled a bit by the way he slid across the big wooden floor between position rehearsals and sat hand in hand with his friend, who was no doubt as charming a youth as you'd wish to meet but not my type.

I'd been there about fifteen minutes when Stephanie saw me. She frowned and then came over.

'Well, hi,' she said, 'this is a surprise. What are you doing in these parts?'

'I phoned your flat,' I said, 'Tarra told me you were here.'

Given time to think about it she became breathlessly surprised. Wasn't it mahvellous to see me again?

'Yeah well, I'm working in Mayfair and I had the afternoon off,' I said.

The director's voice barked across the big gloomy hall:

'*If* you've got a spare bloody moment, Stephanie, sweetness!'

'He's obnoxious as a person,' she said to me, 'but he's a wonderful professional.' She took hold of my hand and then leaned away, making it look as if I was holding on to her. 'We'll be through in half an hour – you will wait, won't you?'

They did a run-through. British Intelligence, played by he of the hairy arms, wasn't too sure if the lovely Wanda, played by Stephanie in a how-you-say-eet-een-Eengleesh accent, was really bringing over the Communist bloc's secret plans or trying to compromise a randy Cabinet Minister.

I made a note to be watching *Come Dancing* that night.

Interesting evening that. We went back to her flat so that she could change. She was flabbergasted to know I wasn't a casino bouncer but a glamorous private detective. I didn't tell her this till we were in the car going up Camden Hill Road to Notting Hill Gate, which is probably why she hadn't introduced me to the celebrities. I suppose it would have been bad for her image, saying 'This is Jim, he was my cruise crew screw.'

When she heard the truth she became quite excited, to the point of telling me what trendy Chelsea restaurant we would go to and what absolutely vibrant discotheque we would rush to afterwards.

I said great only I'd been badly beaten up a couple of nights before and really couldn't be doing with too much exertion, specially as the doc thought I could have blackouts from all those blows to the head.

I'll tell you, I was a better class of actor than anything in that church hall. She said that was terrible and announced that she would cook her speciality paella for me and we could listen to some nice albums and drink some good wine.

They never do admit that it's all down to a good rumping.

Their flat was in Princes Square off Westbourne Grove. Tarra was a sly-eyed richard with coppery hair – dyed – and a dirty laugh. She was going out to dinner with some disgusting freak she couldn't shake off because he was gluey with money.

Stephanie and I were in bed when she came back to the flat with this geezer. I never saw him because they had a drunken shout-up in the sitting-room. He pissed off with a lot of door slamming and she came into Stephanie's bedroom and sat on the bed and told us she would kill herself before she went out with a pig like him again. She was weeping at one stage.

Next thing she was stripping off and getting into the bed. I'd seen off a bottle and a bit of red wine and Stephanie, not much less, so nobody was horrified, although remembering why Tarra's husband got shot of her I didn't risk too much affection.

First time I'd been in a sandwich, funnily enough. Makes the bed very warm.

I got out of there about one o'clock. They were both snoring with their mouths open, a couple of big city beauties living the swinging life.

You wonder I'd spent most of the evening looking forward to the moment when I got a grip on Uncle Sidney?

Chapter Fourteen

The sunshine was pouring down on Horseferry Road when the four of us came out on to the pavement. We were an unlikely quartet but we were all looking very happy with each other.

Happy? Mrs Spencer looked as if she could have gone straight to Caxton Hall registry office and married Desperate for the performance he'd put up in the coroner's court.

We walked up to Victoria Street. Uncle Sidney was giving Mrs Spencer some light chat. You'd have been hard put to it to remember he was largely responsible for her husband's death. I was looking for a place to delve out the readies.

'Just a minute,' I said when we came to Abbey Orchard Street.

'Don't worry, we won't run away,' said Uncle Sidney with a laugh as I took her into the side street.

I was well pleased to be finishing my business with that woman. Right up to the last she'd shown her usual eagerness to hold on to her cash. It was just crossing my mind she might still be planning a flanker. The coroner had given his verdict of death by misadventure and she might have thought she could now get away with not paying anybody.

I was ready to tell her how Desperate might chop off her ears but from her handbag she pulled a white envelope.

'I thought Mr Cooper did very well,' she said, handing me the readies.

'Yeah he did.' I tore open the envelope. 'All here, is it?'

'Two hundred pounds – that's right, isn't it?' she said, looking at me and then the money with the sad widow look.

'Yeah. Let's pay them off.'

As we walked back I thumbed six fivers off the bundle. That

was Desperate's thirty, to make up the fifty he'd been promised.

We were back in a foursome on the broad pavement of Victoria Street when I realized my mistake. I should have nailed her back there for my money.

I gave the thirty quid to Desperate.

'Sorry about all this, Mrs Spencer,' said Uncle Sidney, smiling sadly, 'but we wasn't to know, was we? We ain't bad chaps, just that we was doin' our usual thievin' about the West End an' your husband happened to git his wires crossed. Really sorry, ain't we, Desp?'

'Yeah, tough,' said the big, pock-marked man, already squinting impatiently up the street for a taxi.

Mrs Spencer got in first. She saw the taxi coming from Parliament Square before Desperate. She got to the kerb with her arm out.

'Thank you again,' she said, looking back at us. The taxi pulled in.

I walked over and got hold of her arm. Behind me Copeland said something to Desperate.

'There's the sixty quid you still owe me,' I said to her.

'Oh,' she said, eyes going wide, 'I forgot all about that. I was so nervous about the inquest.'

'You want this cab or donchyer, lady?' said the driver.

'Yeah, okay – I'll give you a ring tomorrow,' I said, letting her go.

Uncle Sidney gave me an impatient look.

'Well thanks again for the little bit ov business,' he said. 'You got somethin' for me, ain't yer?'

'Yeah but I'd like a chat with you,' I said.

Desperate saw a taxi coming up on the other side from Victoria Station. He gave it a roar.

'Look, I done wot you asked,' Uncle Sidney snapped, 'just bung us me readies will yer? Desp an' me's got a meet up Soho.'

'No, I need a chat with you.'

'Come on, Sid, I gotta cab,' Desperate shouted from the middle of the street.

'Comin',' Copeland called. To me he snarled, 'Don't push yer fakkin luck, son.'

'I got the money,' I said, letting him see it in my fist, 'but you and me's got more business.'

'I don't want no more fakkin business.'

'You got no option, Uncle Sidney.'

'Who says so? You want me to git Desp back here to thump you one?'

'Simon Coddington says so,' I said calmly.

Like a kick in the cobblers it must have been. His face almost slid to the pavement.

From the cab on the other side Desperate's big face peered out of the window.

'Come on, Sid, we're in a bleedin' hurry,' he bawled.

I gave Uncle Sidney a pat on the shoulder. The bounce had gone right out of him.

Desperate shouted something else. Uncle Sidney shrugged his shoulders and raised his palms.

'I'll see yer up there,' he shouted.

Desperate gave him a two-finger salute and sat back in the cab, which pulled away in the direction of Big Ben.

'Good job you weren't relying on him for help,' I said.

'He's copped his bunce money, hunnee?' said Uncle Sidney quietly, 'he'd abandon his own mother inna Sahara Desert for a drink-up.'

'Let's find a boozer and get you a seat before I give you the good news,' I said. He shrugged.

'I'm fated.'

We went up Tothill Street on the other side of Victoria Street and found a natty little corner pub with several bars. We went into the one marked Private Lounge. It was empty except for a boxer dog curled in front of the coal fire.

'Scotch,' he said. He sat at a table, his mouth turned down, his eyes watching me wearily. I went to the jump. It was a dark room with wooden panelling and old-fashioned furniture that

145

was almost black. Copeland's small, ruddy face was like something from an old painting.

After leaning over the jump and coughing and whatnot I got one of the barmen from the busy bars to come round. I took the drinks back to the table.

'We've met before of course,' I said, sitting opposite him.

'Course we have. I seem to be doin' nuffin else but meetin' you. I wish I'd niver clapped fakkin eyes on yer.'

'No – we met before this caper. I knew you as Simon Coddington then – the man who abandoned ship at Gibraltar. You still don't remember me?'

He looked at me with pained eyes. I thought he was liable to be sick. I smiled. He swallowed. It was cruel what I was doing to him.

'I was the plant on that boat,' I said. 'I'm an enquiry agent. The cruise company wanted to find out why there was a leak in the casino till. Remember that actress you were trying to chat up?'

He just stared at me. I took a sip of lager. He didn't touch the glass of scotch. His hands were on the table.

'You surprised me when you jumped ship,' I went on. 'I had my eye on the girl – Jennifer Carmichael? I didn't realize you were a double-act.'

'It was that long streak ov piss that was watchin' her,' he said. He frowned, examining my face. 'Yeah, I do remember you now. Shit! So wot's the score now then?'

'First off – here's your dough,' I said, sliding the hundred and fifty across polished wood.

'Knowin' you it's likely poisoned,' he said bitterly, letting it lie beside his hands. 'So wot else do you know, you bastard?'

'Isn't that enough?' I decided not to tell him I knew about the house in Twickenham. For the moment he was on the rails but that wouldn't last long. Six or seven aces up your sleeve was what you needed to stay alive in his game.

'Wot you want from me now then?' he demanded.

'A confession. How you worked the oracle with Jennifer Carmichael. Just cough the lot, that's all I want.'

'Confession? You fakkin jokin'?' He snorted. Life was slowly creeping back into his veins. 'Confessin' ain't wot I do, me old son.'

'This time it is. I take it The Enemy doesn't know a thing, eh?'

This time his eyes were more like normal. Shrewd.

'You can't pull that one on me again,' he said. 'There ain't no room in Rosenau Street any more – an' that spastic geezer don't remember a thing about it, I promise you that.'

'All right then, shall I just scream for the law and hand you over? We could stroll into Scotland Yard right now, if you want it that way.'

'But you ain't got anythin' on me!'

'Oh no? False passport? Conspiracy to defraud? Embezzlement? Plenty of witnesses to say you were on board the SS *Apollo* as Simon Coddington and that you were winning a bundle at the Aussie girl's table? The false passport and fake name should be pretty good evidence you were conspiring with her to weed out the casino takings. Jumping ship with her? She's lodged fake references to get the job in the first place? You know where she is, by the way?'

He shook his head quickly.

'Well,' I said, 'the Old Bill can pick her up easy enough. She'll put it all down to you, I expect. Yes, your honour, he pretended to be a rich man and I fell for him and then he corrupted me, the swine, and made me help him swindle the cruise company . . . with your record, Uncle Sidney? She'll get the pity and you'll get the porridge.'

He covered his eyes with his hand and groaned. He waited, head down, for me to speak. I took a sip of lager. He came up slowly.

'It weren't like that at all,' he said. 'I swear to God. If I tell you!'

'I wish you would.'

He swallowed.

'All right. I'll tell yer. I've put by some loot over the years, haven't I? Only with my trouble and strife, The Enemy, Vera,

God rot her, wot chance do I git for a bit ov enjoyment? Can't make a move, can I, not wiv her an' all her bleedin' family breathin' down my neck. So I come up wiv this bright idea ov gittin' a false passport to do a bit of duckin' and divin' in places she nor her bleedin' brovvers an' cousins'll suss me out. A cruise, like. Plenty of grumble and grunt on these boats, innair? That's for Siddenay. So I'm on that tub an' wot happens? This girl lets me chat her up and sure enuff, soon I'm givin' her a right seein' to in her cabin. Then she says she's got a sick Mum back home in Aussie land an' she'd dearly like to git some loot to send home only they don't hardly pay them anythin' like decent wages. Now – if she could deal me winnin' cards I could pick up a bundle at her table an' we could split it after. I don't tell her I'm S. Copeland, Esquire, workin' the boards in Oxford Street, do I? She thinks I'm in the used car racket, stinkin' wiv money. So I think, well, bit ovva wheeze, innit? Who's to know? Only if I don't help her somebody else will an' bang goes my bit ov crumpet for the cruise. So we do it once an' pick up four or five tons. Then this lanky berk on the casino staff gits all busy snoopin' round her table an' she says we've bin rumbled. I can't take no chances of bein' collared for that caper, can I? Not wiv a bent passport an' brovvers-in-law who'd dance on me skull if I did the dirty on their precious bleedin' Vera. So we git on our toes when the boat's hit Gibraltar. We fly back to London an' wave bye bye an' that's it. Till you've come bargin' in.' He took a quick drink of scotch. His eyes never left my face. 'An' that's the story, God's truth, on my movver's grave.'

'Oh?' I said, sitting back. 'That explains the ticket.'

'Wot ticket?'

'I couldn't see how you could nick enough to cover the eight hundred you paid for the cruise.'

'That was me own gelt – I didn't go on no bleedin' cruise to chop into the takin's, did I? I went to git myself a bit ov the sweet things in life. Now you wanna fit me up for conspiracy! It's a diabolical liberty, that's what it is.'

'Yeah,' I said sympathetically. I shook my head. 'Landed

yourself right in it, didn't you? Sorry about that. But what can I do – unless . . .'

'Yeah?' he said eagerly.

'No – in my racket I couldn't take the risk.'

'Much they payin' you, Jim?' he said quickly. 'Look, I still gotta bit tucked away, I can make it up to yer.'

'No, it isn't the money,' I said doubtfully, 'I got that job through a big agency, 'less I give them something they won't be hiring me again. I got to give them something. Just a minute –'

He leaned forward, his sharp little eyes missing none of the changing emotions going across my honest face.

'She's the one,' I exclaimed. 'If I could chuck her at them . . .'

'Yeah!'

'But you don't know where she is, you said.'

'Ah.' He tapped his nose and winked. 'That's wot I said. Mibbe I got an idea where she can be found.' He took a bigger gulp of scotch. 'In fact, I'm sure ovvit. Listen, Jim, I help you fit her up, you can keep my name out ovvit, can yer? She told me the whole story, the other trips she done, the lot!'

'Yeah but you'd have to make a statement at least – maybe even give evidence. Still – you could do that as Simon Codding-ton, couldn't you? The Enemy doesn't have to connect you with it.'

'That's it! Long as you're willin' to forget you know who I am really – I'll say I went turtles over this smashin' young bird and she sweet-talked me into this caper an' tricked me wiv her feminine wiles. Yeah, triffic! Listen, I'll just go to the carsi and then we'll do some schemin'.'

'Uh uh,' I said, shaking my head. We both went through to the lavatory. Standing next to each other I said, 'She could get weighed off for half a stretch out of this, you don't mind?'

He grinned.

'Fakk her rotten luck,' he said, giving it a shake and zipping up, 'she's crooked, ain't she?'

He gave me a big wink. I looked down.

That's when he gave me the slip. He was through the carsi

door and off, leaving me in mid-stream. I started after him but couldn't stop the flow quick enough.

By the time I got to the pavement he was gone.

You think I hadn't been expecting something of the sort? From Uncle Sidney? Don't be naïve. That's why I hadn't told him I knew about the house in Twickenham. I hadn't wanted him to give me the slip but now it had happened I was pretty sure of his next move. I got to the car and drove down Victoria Street and into Buckingham Palace Road, heading west for Twickenham where Uncle Sidney thought he would be safe, down there among the big hedges and the posh neighbours.

The funny thing was, around then I began to feel just a bit sorry for him. He was a thieving little bastard but you had to admire his cheek.

Not to mention his energy!

Chapter Fifteen

It was two o'clock before he showed in the yellow Jensen.

I was sitting in the Stag fifty yards up the avenue. The Jensen turned into the opening in the big laurel hedge. I gave him a couple of minutes to get in the house and then I switched on the engine and drove slowly down to his gate.

The Jensen was out of sight in the garage. I stopped where the hedge blocked his view of the road. I got out and walked round the hedge and up the short drive to the front door. I could see he wasn't a keen gardener. Everything was coming up weeds.

The door had a fancy knocker in the shape of a gargoyle's face. I let it drop a couple of times. Nobody came.

I walked round past the closed garage door and through to the flower beds and big lawn at the back. I kept close to the wall and then peeped in the french windows.

He was on the phone in the big drawing-room.

I drew my head back and waited. When I looked again he was putting the phone down. I stepped out in full view and rapped on the glass. When he looked across I put my thumbs to my ears and stuck out my tongue.

I couldn't hear what he said but I knew what his lips were saying.

His shoulders fell.

I pointed to the handle. He started towards the windows, then hesitated. The sun was at my back and I could see into the big room quite clearly. I saw him looking quickly at a brown paper carrier-bag on a big fawn sofa.

He came to the windows and mouthed something at me, pointing to the lock and shrugging. He had no key. He wanted me to go round to the front door. I gave him a thumb-up and walked away from the window.

Then I tip-toed back. He was standing in the middle of the room, the carrier-bag in his right hand, looking round desperately. He looked inside a big black piano with its lid up. That didn't suit him. He slid open the door of a fitted cupboard beside the stone fireplace.

Then he went to a high-backed armchair in the far corner. He knelt on the chair and lowered the bag into the corner. He stood back and looked at it from all angles. He pushed the chair nearer the corner.

Then he went to the door.

I hurried round to the front of the house. When he opened the front door I gave him a nod and a wink.

'You'll go a long way for a piss,' I said.

All he could say was:

'Fuck my old boots!'

Give Copeland credit, he still wasn't admitting defeat. He took me into the big lounge with the french windows.

'You're harder to lose than athlete's foot you are,' he exclaimed. 'Don't tell me how you noo about this gaff.'

'Followed you here as well, didn't I?' I said. I looked round. 'Nice. Cost you a few bob I should imagine.'

'Cost *me*? Nah. It ain't *mine*.' He stood and stared at me, shaking his head. 'Might as well have a drop of scotch,' he said. 'You're hauntin' me, you are.'

'Yeah. Nothing to drink for me, thanks, I never know where I might have to rush next to keep up with you.'

He sighed and made an apologetic grimace.

'You honestly expect me to do anythin' different?'

'Not really. This isn't your place you say?'

'Nah.' He went to the cupboard with the sliding door. The drinks were in there. He pulled out a bottle of Glen Grant and two glasses. I shook my head. He put one of the glasses back and then poured himself a big one. 'You might as well know all my horrible little secrets now I s'pose. It's this rich bird I'm knockin' off, she belongs to all this. She's a right old bag but she's loaded.'

'I see.'

'That's why I had the room in Battersea – this one don't know I'm on the three-card caper, she thinks I'm guvnor of my own business in Essex. So I have to be togged out in good gear for her, don't I? Only wot's Vera goin' to think if I'm never done slopin' off in high-class clobber?'

'And this rich woman pays for the car and the cruises and the suits and that?'

'Yeah! Dropped right into it here I have. Perfeck set-up – till you come bargin' in.'

'Well well, Uncle Sidney, you're a right goer for a man of your age I'll give you that.'

'I ain't so old,' he said indignantly. 'I'm only forty-nine.'

He caught my eye. He laughed.

'Fifty-five?' I said.

'If I tell you. Swear to God. Fifty-three, God's my witness.'

'I believe you. So let's just get it straight. You're working the boards in Oxford Street with Desperate and Bungalow and the chaps. They know you as Sidney Copeland from Stamford Hill, where you've got a wife called Vera The Enemy. You pick up this rich bag and pretend you're in a good line of business in Essex. She goes a bundle on you and forks out all the dough you need. To help matters you take that room in Battersea for changing in – I suppose you duck out the back way just in case Vera's put any of the family on your trail?'

'You got it, Jim. Cor, you're sharp, me old son, I'd niver have given you credit first time I met you.'

'Just out of interest – how do you explain to Vera why you're away so much?'

'I've got annuver three-card team workin' the South Coast, haven't I? Each time I come home I bung her a few quid an' that keeps her happy. An' I've warned her not to mention a dicky-bird about it to Desperate or Bungalow or they'll want to move in.'

'But you haven't got another three-card team doing the South Coast?'

'Course not. I hardly got time to fakkin breathe!'

'So on the strength of this rich lady's lolly you go for a little

153

cruise on your faked passport and happen to chat up Jennifer Carmichael, who turns out to be a bent dealer herself?'

'Couldn't believe it myself when she's told me.'

'The passport?'

'Bloke I know gits them for everybody. You git a photograph an' a copy of some dead geezer's birth certificate – s'easy.'

'On this cruise Carmichael talks you into helping her swindle the casino? Then she realizes she's been sussed so you both have to jump ship?'

'That's it.'

'She's frightened of being collared and you don't want anybody investigating your background as Simon Coddington?'

'Yeah.'

'I see.'

He was sitting on the edge of the big fawn sofa, elbows on knees, bald head reflecting the sunshine from the french windows. He was wearing a clean white shirt but apart from that he was in his Oxford Street scruff gear.

'Well it's all very fascinating,' I said, 'but the only bit I'm interested in is the ship. As long as I know you weren't part of any kind of syndicate swindling the cruise company –'

'God's my witness.'

'Then all I want from you is the statement putting it all down to Jennifer Carmichael. You can come with me to the cruise company's office in Lombard Street. I only know you as Simon Coddington, right? Chances are they might not even want to prosecute Jennifer Carmichael – as long as they're sure they know how it was done and how to stop it happening again. They did find out there was no Simon Coddington at the address you gave but we can get round that.'

'I'll say I sneaked off on the cruise without the wife knowin' an' didn't want any letters goin' to my home she might git her hands on.'

'Very good. So the big thing is – where's Jennifer Carmichael?'

He pointed his index finger at me and showed me his teeth.

'I can probably help you there, Jim. All her papers was fakes an' that but she told me where she hangs out normally – in

Bournemouth, I even know her kosher name. Sylvia Groombridge. She ain't even Australian, just bin out there a coupla year. It'll be easy nuff to dig her out in Bournemouth, she owns a flat in a posh block, I'll remember the name ov it in a minute.'

'Gets better and better, Uncle Sidney. I don't see you coming out of this too badly after all.'

He grinned enthusiastically.

'One thing they're bound to hammer at,' I said. 'You quite sure that five hundred quid she made you win that night playing pontoon was the only loot you had out of the casino?'

'I didn't even have that,' he said, indignantly. 'She had that five tons, she did. I mean, I was supposed to be stinkin' wiv money, wasn't I? I didn't have a penny out of it, God's truth.'

'That's okay then.' I leaned back and put my hands behind my neck and yawned. Suddenly I stiffened up. 'That somebody at the door?'

He cocked his head.

'Didn't hear nuffin,' he said.

'Yeah – definitely, there was somebody at the front door.'

He got up and left the room. I got on one knee on the chair and stretched my right arm down into the corner.

When he came back into the room I had the carrier-bag open and was throwing bundles of notes on to the Persian carpet.

'She loves you, she loves you not, she loves you, she loves you not . . .'

They were slim wads, some of tenners and some of twenties, not new notes, each wad held by a fancy paper-clip.

There was at least thirty or forty thousand in the bag.

I looked up at Copeland and said:

'Your rich fancy woman planning to paper the room with faces of the Queen, is she?'

This time he looked near to tears.

But you know what they say about rats when the wall is at their backs.

First he tried to tell me he had no idea that much money was lying about the house.

I told him I'd seen him hiding the bag, which was why I'd kidded him on there was somebody at the door.

Then he said it was his rich fancy woman's cash, which she was too superstitious to trust to the bank.

I said I knew perfectly well his rich old bag was actually Jennifer Carmichael because I'd seen them together at the front of the house the day he skedaddled from Rosenau Street.

Then he said it was his own money, saved up from a lifetime of blagging and fannying suckers.

I said I knew he'd only come into this money a couple of months or so before, around the time the computer was beginning to spot a drop in the ship's casino.

He couldn't think of anything else.

'Okay then, Jim – let's cut out the bollocks – you can have ten grand of this loot for yourself if you'll just piss off an' forget about me.'

I stood up.

'Ten grand?' I said.

'Twelve then – can't be fairer than that, can I?'

'No deal,' I said. 'Where's Carmichael now? She going to be long?'

'I dunno.'

I picked up the bundles from the carpet and dropped them into the carrier-bag.

'I'll just make a phone call then and we can sit and wait for the boys in blue.'

He was silent for a moment.

Then he cleared his throat.

'Look, Jim, I stole that money somewhere else altogether. It ain't got nuffin to do with them ships. I'll cough all you want about the casino caper, sign a statement, anythin' – only I don't wanna be here when Jenny gits back. It'll be too embarrassin' if I'm grassin' on her.' He looked at his watch. 'She'll be back here any time, let's scarper, eh?'

'And lose her? Uh uh.'

'She won't know anythin's up. I'll leave her a message. You

got me money, ain't yer? I'm gonna give yer the slip an' leave forty grand behind, am I?'

I stood there saying nothing. There was no way I could prove this money came from the ships. Unless he was willing to cough I didn't really have much on them at all. So far I'd been threatening him with The Enemy but that hold wasn't going to last much longer.

What I wanted was to get him up to R. K. Brown Cruises Limited in Lombard Street and do some talking before he could find a window to dive out of.

'You do me one favour an' I'm yours for anythin' you want,' he pleaded.

'What favour?'

He brought out the thin wad of fivers I'd given him outside the coroner's court.

'I can't leave Vera with nuffin, can I?' he said. 'You drive me up to Stamford Hill an' let me give her this lot an' I'll go anywhere you like. Ain't too much to ask, is it? You know too well they're goin' to nick me if they can – wot's Vera gonna live on?'

I watched him write out a note to Jennifer Carmichael. Like everything else he did with his small red hands the writing was neat. He said he'd see her in the morning. I watched him every inch of the way. He signed it with the initials S.C. He had no chance to leave her any kind of tip-off.

He left the note on the phone table in the hall.

In case this was a pre-arranged signal I moved it to the hall-stand, sticking it under the wood at the edge of the mirror. He looked at me reproachfully, shaking his head.

Outside the sun was shining. The bag of money wasn't too heavy considering how much it held. I almost threw it up in the air, thinking what a clever bastard I was.

'Your car or mine?' I said.

'Yours, naturally.' He even managed a cheeky smile. 'We drive up our street in a yellow Jensen belongin' to me Vera might git a bit suspicious of her darlin' Siddenay, mightn't she?'

He turned chatty on the drive. He'd worked it out that they couldn't do much to him. I didn't say a lot. He was a likeable little bleeder and I didn't have the heart to remind him that large-scale fraud was worth about five years these days.

It was obvious what would happen. They'd both be charged and then they'd both try to nominate the other for being the master-mind. The judge would cough dryly and send them both down.

'I'm just a petty nobody,' he said, 'all I done was organize a bent passport to have a bit of a lark away from the missus. She's the one wiv the fake references an' that – anybody can tell I'm just a smalltime tea-leaf.'

'On your previous there's an item about a shotgun,' I said. 'Bit out of character for a petty con-man, wasn't it, a shotgun?'

He snorted.

'I was on me way to a weddin', wun I?'

I drove with the money-bag on the floor behind me. He was twisted round in the passenger seat, arm on the back of my seat. Every time we were stopped by the lights I could practically hear him weighing the chances of grabbing the bag and diving out the door but he knew I'd have him by the collar before his hand reached the carrier-bag.

Then we turned into Overlea Road. The sun was in our faces so we were almost at his garden gate before we saw the two men going up his garden path. Parked outside was a powder-blue Jaguar Mark Ten.

He let out a squeak and started scrabbling to get down on the floor.

'Git the fuck outa here!' he squealed. He sounded demented.

I'd been slowing down but I managed to get some speed up without making it too noticeable. As we were passing the blue Jaguar one of the men looked round. It was Billy Bunter Begg.

The other was a tall, thin bloke. They were both wearing dark blue suits.

'Git goin', git the fuck out ovvit!' Uncle Sidney hissed up at me from the floor of the car. His eyes were bright with terror. 'They've rumbled me! Git us outa here for God's sake, they wanna kill me!'

Chapter Sixteen

I came out into the little park and then did a quick right turn into Craven Walk. He kept begging me and then shouting at me to get the hell out of the whole district.

Instead I went down to the bottom of the street and pulled in behind a blue Volkswagen. I looked back but there was nothing coming after us.

'You think they saw me?' he squeaked. His knees were twisted under the dashboard ledge and his bald head was jammed against the upholstery. For the first time I felt I wasn't getting an act.

'Dunno,' I said. 'Begg, wasn't it?'

'Yeah – and the fakkin Dentist! Oh for God's sake – git goin', Jim, he'll kill me on the spot he will!'

'Why?'

'I'll tell yer, honest I will, only we gotta scoot. *Please* – I'll do anythin' you want, only git movin'.'

'Why do you think he's after you?'

'It was his money I nicked, wunnit? Oh God. How the hell did he fakkin find out? I'm a gonner.'

I put my hand on the ignition.

'Okay, I'll start driving if you start telling me the whole story. All right?'

His little fresh face was in agony, although that might have been from the way his legs were twisted under him.

'I'll do anythin' you want, Jim, anythin', only git a move-on for Christ's sake.'

I kept the smile off my face. I didn't see we were in any danger. All they could have seen was a man driving a navy blue Stag up Overlea Road. Begg might have remembered my face from the Wardorf Club only I didn't think he'd got a good look at me passing in the car.

But at last I had Uncle Sidney by the short and curlies.

His terrified face was still staring up at me as I started up and turned right into Ashtead Road.

The powder-blue Jag was coming out into Craven Walk. I had to swing hard to the left to miss it. There were two men in the front but I only got a look at the driver's face.

'That the Dentist?' I said casually. 'The thin bloke with a face like the front of a ship?'

'Don't even talk about him!'

'Only he's just passed us in that big blue Jag,' I said, shooting into Spring Hill and then belting up towards the main road. Uncle Sidney shut his eyes in horror.

'Have you lost 'em?' he moaned.

'Yeah but I can soon find them again if you don't start telling me what it's all about.'

'I will, honest, just let's git a hundred mile away first.'

I craned my neck to look up the length of the little park. There was no sign of the blue Jag.

'There they are,' I said, 'just up there by the hamburger stand. Why's he called the Dentist?'

'Cos he likes pullin' yer teeth out wiv a pair of fakkin pliers, that's why,' moaned Uncle Sidney. 'Oh God, can't yer git the hell away from here?'

'I'll try. Just you start telling me things, I always drive better when I'm listening to something.'

And that was how I dragged the whole story out of him, by putting on a fake car chase. I did a lot of fast cornering and dicey overtaking, taking streets at random, every so often looking in the mirror and making sharp hissing noises.

As far as he was concerned, down there on the floor, the merchants of death were on our tail and I was the only thing between him and a fatal case of bleeding gums.

It was cruel what I did to him and it wasn't a pretty sight, the brave little joker reduced to a shaking wreck, but I wasn't giving up this chance of forcing the truth out of him.

Any time he looked like recovering his nerve and remembering a lifetime rule of telling nobody anything all I had to do was look in the rearview mirror, hiss sharply and shoot round the first corner.

Yeah, cruel.

Still, he'd no doubt see the funny side later on.

'So how did you steal Begg's money?' I wanted to know.

'From his safe deposit. I got hold of his keys, din I? Does it fakkin matter? Can't you git this motor movin' quicker?'

'I want to hear the whole story. From the off.'

'Oh God. Well, it was in November, we was up in the Wardorf, he's well pissed, innee?'

'Who is?'

'Begg! Had a big win or somethin' – not offen you see him pissed. So I go into the carsi and there's this wallet on the floor. I have a quick shufti through it, see if there's anythin' worth nickin' an' spot his safe deposit keys.'

'Do go on,' I snapped, both hands tight on the wheel, crouching forward. We were going back up Ashtead Road only he didn't know that. The sun was shining and a man was painting a gate. Two boys were kicking a ball.

'I noo wot the keys looked like cos my own are the same, inney?'

'Would that be Bullion Stores in Great Portland Street?'

'Yeah. How d'you know that?'

'Never mind. So you just nicked the keys, did you?'

'Course I didn't! He's not that pissed he isn't gonna notice his wallet's missing, is he? Anyway, look, let's lose the bastard then I'll be able to tell yer better.'

I started to slow down.

'Wot you doin' for God's sake?' he squealed.

'I want to know now or I stop this vehicle and open that door and boot you out in the gutter,' I snarled. I glanced in the mirror. 'Oh yeah, here they come.'

'All right, all right,' he gasped. I put my foot down and got her up to forty again. This time I shot through the little park and went left into the main road.

'So how did you know they were Bullion Stores keys?' I asked.

'Cos I got the same myself. That's where I've been bungin' some of me own readies, innit? Nuffin much, just a grand or so, me savin's that The Enemy don't know about. Anyway, I can't nick the keys, he's bound to spot they're on the missin' list soon as he sobers up an' git the safe deposit manager to change his box, innee? Same goes if I half-inch the wallet. Besides that, he'll more or less remember when he last had the wallet an' then start workin' out who all was in the club at the time. If he don't remember his mates will. So I think about it for half a sec an' then I've pressed the keys in the soap, hun I? An impression, like. Then I wipe the keys clean an' drop the wallet back on the floor for the next bloke in the carsi to find an' I wrap the soap up in toilet paper an' bung it in my pocket. Where are they now?'

I looked in the mirror. We were shooting down Lower Clapton Road.

'Can't see 'em,' I said.

'Git into the side streets then, give 'em the slip for God's sake. Then we git back to Twickenham, nobody knows about the house – barrin' you.'

'Oh oh – there they are,' I groaned. 'Keep talking.'

'So there I am wiv Begg's safe deposit keys on soap.' He laughed.

I couldn't believe it – but he laughed. I could see his forehead wrinkling. I put my foot down and took a corner so fast he was pushed against the door. When I straightened up again he had stopped laughing but he had recovered enough to twist around till he could free his legs. He sat there on the floor with his hands clasped round his knees.

'I don't believe a single word you've said,' I snarled. 'Let's stop and see if Billy Bunter'll confirm your fairy story.'

'No – don't do that!' he yelped. 'It's the truth, straight up, God as my witness!'

'You just happened to find his wallet and recognize his safe deposit keys and slap them on to a cake of soap – on the spur of the moment? With a real heavy like him? Don't believe you, mate.'

'At the time I just did it, din I? I mean, you see an openin' you grabs it, donchyer?'

'You might.'

'Think I'd tell you a tale – wiv him breathin' hard on our backs? Nah, I just dived straight in when I saw the chance – it's how I've always been, innit? Just like workin' the three-card caper, that's how you earn, innit, spot the mug an' dive in.'

'Yeah? So what then?'

We were going west on Dalston Lane. I'd decided to head for the City. It seemed a good time to deliver the little shyster to R. K. Brown Ltd. While he was in a talking mood.

'Well, I git this geezer I know to make me replicas of the keys from the soap – they're only ordinary keys, easy enuff to copy. Then I sit tight for a while, thinkin' wot do I do next? I gotta be dead cliver, hun I?' He shook his head, peeping up at me suspiciously. 'I niver thought I'd ever be tellin' all this to a single livin' soul I didn't. You could git me chopped to bits startin' at the eye-teeth, you know that, donchyer?'

'Don't forget it.' I looked in the mirror. 'Maybe we've lost 'em.' I leaned back into the seat and stretched my shoulders. He started to speak but I took my left hand off the wheel and pointed the finger at him. 'Don't start fannying me now – I can get us to Begg's place in Walthamstow double-quick if you try to flannel me. I daresay the Dentist hasn't a lot of time for pain-killing injections and that.'

'Don't use that word killin', *please*, sends shivers up and down me. Look, if we've shook 'em let's git back to the house.'

'Uh uh. We'll go to see the cruise company and you can do your owning up about the casino fiddle.'

'Nah – I'll do it, yeah, but it's gotta be as Simon Coddington, hunnit? I need the wig an' the good gear, doan I? Cos once I tell these people about the ship caper I'm gonna have to dis-appear for ever, ain't I? Even if they turn me over to the Old

Bill I'll stick to sayin' I'm Simon Coddington, won't I? Long as I'm Coddington Begg'll niver know where Sidney Copeland went. So we'll just git over to Twickenham lively like an' pick up me gear an' me passport an' then I'm your man.'

'But you were going to be my man before. We were supposed to be on our way to Lombard Street when we saw Begg at your front door, weren't we? You were only dropping in to give The Enemy the housekeeping money.'

He took a deep breath and squinted up at me. Then he laughed.

'All right, so I was plannin' on givin' you the slip before we ever got to see them cruise people, wun I? Sorry about that. But this time I won't try nuffin clever, on my sacred –'

'Yeah yeah, I believe you. Only don't try anything from now on because first hint of anything dodgy I'm handing you over to Begg, right? He'll pay me five grand reward – maybe I should go straight to him now, eh?'

'Don't make them sick jokes, please.'

I was in Essex Road by then, heading west for Pentonville Road and then Euston. Maybe I would have been better to take him direct to see Mr Barclay at R. K. Brown but without his confession I didn't really have much except a bag of money that actually belonged to a Walthamstow gangster.

I didn't tell Uncle Sidney that.

'Okay then,' I said gruffly, 'I'll take you back there to pick up your clobber. Only tell me how you went about cleaning Begg's safe deposit out.' I looked into the mirror. 'I reckon it's safe for you to show your head now.'

'No thanks, I like it better down here. Anyway, you know the system in them safe deposit places? You goes to reception an' proves your identity an' then they send somebody down wiv you to the strong-room an' hand you over to the security guards. You give him the safe key an' he opens your box for yer. So the next coupla times I'm in there at me own box I work out from the numbers where Begg's box is gotta be. It's about twenny yards away in a different row ov cabinets. So all I gotta figure is how to git the guard to open his instead ov mine – I mean, them guards git to know your face an' wot number it goes wiv, doaney?'

'That would be the snag. How'd you beat it?'

'Ah ha.' He looked up and gave me a wink. Ten minutes before he'd been rigid with the prospect of Begg's private dentist getting to work on his molars with a hammer and chisel.

You can't keep a funny man down for long. Specially not when he can at last tell somebody the story of the greatest triumph of his life.

'You knows enuff now to have me minced into little bits so where's the harm?' he said, as if to convince himself. 'All I gotta do is wait till there's a noo guard. It's happened about three weeks after I've found the keys. Each time I go in I've got Begg's keys in me other pocket hopin' there's a noo guard. This time I see a strange face when they take me down from reception. I've shown them me own keys but soon as I'm in the strong-room behind the big barred door I give him Begg's key. He opens Begg's safe for me. Then he leaves me alone wiv the box. So I open it up and there starin' me inna face is readies like I've niver seen. Talk about open the box! Cor. If I tell you. Swear to God! I couldn't hardly move a muscle for all ov ten seconds. It was beautiful it was. All tens and twenties in bundles of a hundred – elastic bands? He's kinky that Begg, all the bands is the same colour! You credit that? All blue elastic bands! Well well, I thought, you've hit the jackpot this time, Siddenay. Cor!'

'What did you do – dip in for as much as you could stuff in your pockets?'

'Oh no. I had a bag wiv me, didn't I? Be prepared, that's wot they taught us in the Scouts. I just filled me boots, din I? The lot. No point in havin' a nibble at it, he was gonna notice if there was any missin' so I might as well do the job proper like first time off.'

'Much was it?'

'Ninety grand near enuff. So I called the guard an' he locked the safe an' I walked out wiv all Bunter's loot. I went straight to anuvver safe deposit place –'

'Which one?'

'This is comin' hard enuff tellin' you as much wivout givin' away all me secrets – fair do's!'

'With what you paid cash for that house and what's in the bag – and the car and the suits I don't suppose there's much left in it anyway, is there?'

'Nah, it's all in the bag.' He twisted round to look between the seats. Then he looked up at me. I shook my head slowly.

'I'll hold the bag till we get this sorted out,' I said. 'So there you were with ninety grand of Begg's money. I bet you could hardly wait to start enjoying it.'

'If I tell you. Swear to God! But I gotta box dead clever. If I start spendin' half a sheet more'n me normal somebody'll suss me out in a flash. There's Vera. There's Desperate an' Bungalow an' the team – I know them bastards too bleedin' well, they git the slightest notion I've come into big money they're gonna put the bite on me somethin' cruel. An' there's Begg! Not half. Wiv ninety grand missin' he's gonna be tearin' his hair out. I done the wallet pretty cute – I left it on the carsi floor after I've soaped the keys an' some other bloke found it ten minutes later. Begg might or might not remember losin' it for a little while but he knows somebody's got at his keys so he's gonna be all eyes for any geezer spendin' a lot, innee? As I say, I handled it very well, I think you'll agree.'

'Oh you're a Brain of Britain, you are. We're getting near Marble Arch now, shouldn't think he's likely to be in these parts, you can get up if you like.'

'You got any shades or that?'

I gave him the dark glasses from the glove-box. He put them on and then began to slide-up on to the seat. His legs had gone to sleep and he started groaning and moaning like an old woman. But a little bit of pain wasn't going to interfere with his moment of glory.

'Yeah well. I took it nice an' easy, didn't I? First off I gits up a story for Vera an' her rotten family. Family? Bruvvers, cousins, uncles – she's got more relations than Bugs Bunny, she has. Every one of 'em would cut yer throat for half a nicker!

An' if they thought I was two-timin' their lovely sister Vera they'd do it for gornish! That's how come I invent this other three-card mob I'm runnin' in Bournemouth, innit? That gits me the odd weekend away. Only it's odds on that won't hold up for too long. Then I gits the idea of a bent passport under anuvver name – so's I can do a slippery for a whole week somewhere they'll nivver be. Then I think – I need another gaff! Somewhere posh they've niver heard of. So I think ov Richmond or somewhere like that, ovver end of town. That's how I git the house in Twickenham. I can't rent it cos they need references an' that – the same goes for mortgages so I bung down cash. You shoulda seen the agent's face when I say I wanna pay cash. He says, Yeah, mate, we'll take your cheque. I say, No, mate, I said cash an' I mean cash. So I bung down thirty-five grand or so ov Bunter's loot on his desk.'

He looked round at me quickly. He slapped my arm.

'Go on – say it.'

'Okay,' I said, 'you're taking a big chance the money isn't bent? Hot? Numbered notes from some bank raid or that?'

He slapped my arm again.

'You're bright, Jim, I'll give yer that.' He sighed. 'Pity you hadn't been drowned at birth, you busy bastard. Anyway, I give 'em a coupla days then phone up. If they've sussed the gelt is hot I'm ready just to swallow it – they only know me as Simon Coddington, doaney? But they say it's all hunky-dory so I own the property. Triffic! I can take young birds down there for dirty weekends, can't I? Live like a king – at the weekend anyway.'

'Fantastic. But wouldn't it have saved a lot of aggro just disappearing altogether? You had enough to go anywhere in the world.'

'Oh yeah? I disappear soon after Begg's loot goes missin'? That puts me down as number one probable, dunnit? No, I'm a thinker, Jim, although I say it myself. Wot I've got to do is act natural an' wait me moment. Most of yer villains trips up trynna spend the loot too quick. So I stick wiv the three-card caper an' hang about like normal. I tell Vera I've got this ovver team workin' the South Coast only I don't want Desperate an' Bungalow an' the chaps in on that one – every Monday mornin' I come home I bung her half a hundred or so an' she's happy to keep me secret.'

'What was the room in Battersea all about then?'

'Just extra caution. If any ov 'em gits nosey an' follow me on a Friday night wot'll they find? Me keepin' a little gaff in Battersea? Sorta thing blokes do, innit, keep a little flat on the side for a bit of sparetime grumble?'

We were going west on Cromwell Road, passing the air terminal. I felt in my pockets for my fags. When he saw the packet he screwed up his face.

'Do you mind?' he said. 'That's a habit wot'll kill you, Jim. Can't you do wivout them for a bit?'

'Sod you.'

'So I'm doin' nicely an' then I come up wiv the idea of a cruise,' he said, rolling down his window and making a bit of a show of breathing the outside air. 'Big mistake that was.'

'You'd never met Jennifer Carmichael before, really?'

'Nah! All I'm looking for is somethin' to get a grip on. First off I fancied that black-haired bit, the actress. She –'

'Funny enough, I saw her last night.'

'Oh well, can't win 'em all, can yer? I do remember now, you was buyin' her a drink that night Jennifer got me at it wiv her dodgy dealin'.' He gave my arm a pat. 'Niver mind all this aggravation, she's been worth it! Cor. She's a real raver, Jennifer. She's a nutter on the job, Jim, cor! A night wiv her puts ten years on yer!'

'Could be tricky – at your age.'

'Shut up! She says I'm the business. Honest. Mind you, just as well I only sees her at weekends. Rest of the five days I'm convalescin'.' He started to laugh. Then it turned into a coughing fit. 'Can't you finish that horrible cigarette?' he croaked.

'I'll give up smoking in a minute. So you and this Carmichael bird decide you can't live without each other and you bring her back to your suave mansion in Twickenham? She know you're really Uncle Sid the three-card king?'

'Not exackly. She thinks I'm a big noise in the car game in Essex.'

'Where does she think you spend all the time you're not with her?'

'Wiv me wife an' family ov course. I'd divorce me wife like a shot only we're devout Caffolicks, ain't we? Oh dear, I'm a horrible little liar, really I am.'

'You're a bleeding hero at your age,' I said. 'You've nicked a top gangster's gelt, you're ducking and diving from your real wife, you're keeping up one home in Stamford Hill, a room in Battersea and a love nest in Twickenham. Plus you're still working the three-card trick in Oxford Street. What do you get up to in your spare time?'

'Tell you straight, you ever seen them jugglers on the circus? That's wot it feels like. All them balls in the air and me hopin' I don't drop one cos if I do sure as Laurel loves Hardy *some-body*'s gonna creep up behind an' slit me fakkin gizzard! See those two you had a run-in wiv – Mel and Colly? Them's Vera's nephews. Good blokes – if they're on your side. But if they noo wot I was doin' to their precious Aunt Vera they'd use me stomach for trampoline practice.'

'All because you found a wallet on the carsi floor, eh?'

'Yeah. Ain't life peculiar?' He shuddered. 'Only it don't look so clever now, do it? How the fakkin hell did Begg tumble to me?'

'It was him who had that night guard done over, I suppose.'

'Oh yeah. Obvious, wunnit? His gelt goes for a stroll but there's no break-in. Either gotta be one ov the staff or anuvver key-holder, hunnit? So he wasn't plannin' to break in, he was tryin' to find out how anybody else could've got at his box. It said in the papers, they was beatin' that bloke an' asking all sorts of questions. Like where was the list of key-holders kept. Everybody thinks they're askin' that cos they only want to break into the right boxes, the big bookmakers an' that but wot they're really after is to see a name that could've been near Begg's keys.'

'Like yours.'

'Yeah. He sees my name on the list wot's the first thing he

170

thinks? Wasn't Copeland in the Wardorf that day I was pissed an' dropped me handbag on the carsi floor? You can bet he don't make a habit of droppin' his treasure all round the shop.' He snapped his fingers. 'Buy a paper next chance we see. Odds on that's it.'

The next vendor we saw was at Hammersmith Broadway. We were heading for the bridge. I pulled in to the side. The vendor was across the road. I opened the door. Then I looked at him. We both smiled. I reached down behind the seat and lifted the carrier-bag.

'Suspicious bastard,' he said.

'Sorry about that,' I replied, pulling the ignition key out of the dashboard. I waited for a gap in the traffic and ran across. I brought back one of each. He dived at the *Evening News*. I started the engine and we headed across the bridge.

'Yeah, just as I thought,' he said grimly. 'Had to be, dinnit? Lissen. Second Raid Flop By The Second Rate Gang.' He groaned. 'Begg'll love that – second rate? He thinks he's top man.'

'What does it say?'

He cleared his throat. At the time it didn't seem unusual to hear him speaking in a BBC voice. The time was passed when Uncle Sidney's talents could surprise me.

'For the second time in three months a gang tried to break into a West End safe deposit strong-room early this morning. And again they came away empty-handed. When staff reported for duty at the Great Portland Street offices of Bullion Stores this morning they found doors smashed and offices ransacked. Detectives think it was the same gang who in December beat up a night guard from the same company. On that occasion their haul was the same – nothing. Said a Bullion Stores spokesman, they must be amateurs. And when they found out they couldn't get into the safe deposit boxes they must have blown their tops and taken revenge by breaking up everything in sight. Papers were scattered all over, desk lamps smashed, typewriters thrown about. Still, they didn't crack the strong-room and that's the important thing.'

He held the paper up to give me a look.

'I'm driving this car,' I said.

'Yeah well. He's gone in there last night an' this time he's got wot he was after. Soon as he sees my name on the list of key-holders he's gone straight up to Stamford Hill. I do hope he hasn't given Vera the treatment. One ov her best features, her teeth.' He snorted. 'Nah, she don't know nuffin. Bin nice knowin' yer, Vera.' He looked at me. 'You knows I can niver go back there again, donchyer? Tangle wiv Begg an' you end up a floatin' voter – yeah, one ov the don't knows floatin' up an' down the Thames.'

'I can't see you'll be floating with concrete socks on, baby.'

'Cor, leave me out!' he moaned. 'Lissen, couldn't we forget this ship crap? I stand to git the chop, doan I? Wot's a small fiddle to that?'

'Yeah well, you make sure you don't slide off and I'll make sure they don't give you a fitting for concrete socks. Funny enough I believe your story. Pity you had to pick on the one bent dealer in the whole fleet though.'

'Done now, innit? So wot's the score?'

'You help me get your girlfriend up to Lombard Street. Tell her the game's up but there probably won't be any charges if she owns up and repays the money?'

'Yeah?'

'No but tell her that. You don't mind her getting sent down, do you?'

'Rather her than me.'

'Nobody could call you a sentimental fool. Look – first thing she'll think of is running. You know where she keeps her passport?'

'Her three passports you mean. Yeah, they're in a drawer in the bedroom.'

'Collar them soon as we get there and slip 'em to me. Better give me yours as well.' I flashed my teeth at him. 'Just so's I can trust you a hundred per cent.'

'Cor. I had it made till you turned up. The dream ov a life-time it was – somethin' that made all them rotten years worthwhile. Why couldn't you have taken up an honest line of work, you bastard?'

We got to the house in Twickenham around five. I parked in the road, the drive being taken up with the yellow Jensen and a white Scimitar GTE that he said was hers. We got out of the Stag.

'You think she'll do what you tell her?' I asked.

He looked at the windows, still wearing my shades.

'She ain't so brilliant as she thinks. Fall for any old yarn I spin her she will.'

'Like the way you fell for my yarn about Begg chasing us?' I said. He turned quickly and glared at me. 'Yeah – I lost him right at the beginning in Craven Walk.'

His mouth fell open.

'You –'

'I've learned a lot from you, Uncle Sidney,' I said, lifting out the money bag.

'You mean Begg wasn't followin' us? You rotten bastard!'

'You'd have preferred a real chase would you? It can always be arranged, remember.'

'You bastard.'

'You just get me her passports and tell her what's wanted, all right?'

'King hell! Yeah, all right. Only –' he glanced quickly at the windows again and lowered his voice – 'she knows me as Simon Coddington so we'll forget Uncle Siddenay from now on. Fact of the matter I think the world has seen and heard the last ov Uncle Siddenay.'

'You play ball with me and I'll play with yours.'

He stared at me for a moment.

'You're wasted in your job, you are. You can tell lies better'n I can.'

'I wish I could have that in writing,' I said, our shoes crunching on gravel as we went towards the front door porch.

When Jennifer Carmichael opened the door her face tried

several expressions at once. She knew exactly where she'd last seen me.

'You've been playing hard to get,' I said. 'Can we have that drink now?'

Chapter Seventeen

'Jesus Christ!' said the luscious girl dealer from Down Under.

'Nah, it's Jim Hazell,' said Uncle Sidney cheerily. 'Remember him from the *Apollo*?'

'Too bloody right I remember him,' she snapped. She was wearing a sleeveless purple t-shirt over a maroon blouse, flared trousers with horizontal stripes in orange and red and no shoes. Since I'd last seen her she'd taken to frizzing up her auburn hair. Apart from her face she looked a treat.

There was nothing wrong with her face, either, only what it was doing. For a moment she looked sick. Then she started getting angry.

'Why the bloody hell you have to bring him here?' she snapped at Uncle Sidney.

He put his arm round her shoulder and turned her into the hall. His bald head was an inch short of her frizzy hair. I closed the door. It had a mortice lock, a Yale lock and a chain. I turned the mortice key and put it in my pocket.

I put the carrier-bag down beside the phone table.

'I'm going to make a call,' I said to their backs. They both turned. His arm was still on her shoulder but she didn't look too affectionate. 'I'd like you both to hear it.'

'What's this all about?' she demanded, looking at Uncle Sidney or Simon.

'Don't panic, darlin',' he said, patting her shoulder. She made a slight movement to avoid his hand.

I had to take my eyes off them to dial R. K. Brown's number. I put my foot on the bag. When I heard it ringing I leaned back against the wall and watched them both. Maybe Uncle Sidney was beginning to realize that he'd panicked too easily.

I got through to Mr Barclay's secretary without too much trouble. Jennifer Carmichael didn't know who I was calling but Uncle Sidney did. I kept my eyes on her.

'I'm afraid Mister Barclay is travelling down to Southampton by car,' the secretary said. 'I don't know his movements when he gets there. But he'll be in the office tomorrow morning.'

'I can't ring him anywhere now?'

'He wasn't even sure if he was staying the night. I could try the ship he's going to.'

'Okay. Could you tell him or leave a message that James Hazell rang and that I've got something for him on the *Apollo* job. He knows who I am. I'd like to bring two people to see him in the morning – one of them is Jennifer Carmichael. All right?' She glanced at Uncle Sidney. He could only shrug.

'Jennifer Carmichael?' said Barclay's secretary. 'I don't know if he's free in the morning, actually, he –'

'You tell him the names, he'll be free. Better tell him to get the company lawyer there as well.'

'Can you tell me what it's about exactly, I –'

'Sorry – but Mister Barclay will know. Cheers.'

I put down the phone.

'All right if I go upstairs to the carsi?' said Uncle Sidney. 'Only I'm burstin'.'

He went up the carpeted stairs. I picked up the carrier-bag.

'That was R. K. Brown,' I said to her, not too brutally, 'I hate to be corny but the game is up as it happens. I think you'd better let me have the car keys – both lots.'

'Why should I? What the hell's the idea?'

'You're beautiful when you're angry. The idea is I've traced you both and now you're going to have an owning up session with Mister Barclay of R. K. Brown Cruises Limited. Simon Coddington up there has already told me most of it so don't bother fannying me. You can either do it my way or I can pick up that phone and call the local police station.'

'I don't know what you're talking about,' she said.

'I'll let him tell you. Where are the car keys? I don't want to have to let down tyres or anything.'

'They're in the drawer,' she snapped, nodding at the hall-stand. I walked past her and opened the drawer. I put both sets in my trouser pocket. I could smell her perfume. Or maybe it was soap. Like flowers.

'Any chance of a cold drink?' I said, looking down at her. I showed her my teeth. 'You got any Fosters in the fridge – sport?'

She didn't go a bundle on my Aussie accent. If looks could kill? She slayed me anyway. I hated to think of her in a women's prison. She was lovely. What was she doing cased up with a small bald cockney in his fifties? Even if he was supposed to be Simon Coddington, a rich Essex car-dealer with youthful ambitions, I couldn't see why a cracker like her needed that kind of deal. She was obviously pretty bright and she had a tough edge to her and that's not usually the kind who settle for stray week-ends and lonely weeks by the phone waiting for Sugar Daddy to sneak a call.

'I suppose we *could* stand here all night in the lobby,' I said.

She turned. I followed her through a darkish corridor with a low beam to the big lounge with the french windows.

'I'll get you a drink from the kitchen,' she said, going to the other door.

'Mind if I tag along?'

She gave me a can of Long Life from the fridge. I sat on a bench seat at a big wooden table. 'Cheers,' I said, gurgling on the can. I needed a jimmy riddle but I wasn't going to leave her alone till Uncle Sidney brought me the passports.

She could still do a hotman's on me even then but without the passports she couldn't go very far. And they would have a photograph of her.

'Nice house this,' I said, looking round the big sunny kitchen.

'Glad you like it,' she said sarcastically. I was glad when Uncle Sidney came downstairs. Only now he was Simon Coddington – wig, mohair suit and all. We got up and went into the lounge. She went first. I tapped his shoulder. He looked round. I held out my hand. He made a little face as if he'd forgotten all about the passports. Then he handed them to me. I counted four and put them inside my jacket.

She wouldn't sit down. I took the big sofa. Lovely job it was, so wide your knees were tight against the edge and so high your feet were almost off the floor.

Alias Coddington gave her the story.

'This bastard recognized me in the street,' he said. 'He's a private detective, curse his rotten fakkin hide. You know I can't stand bein' given a spin by the Old Bill so we got no choice. He says we ain't likely to git charged if we make a full statement an' bung back the loot.'

'I don't know what you're talking about,' she snapped. Alias Coddington sat on the arm of an easy chair. He gave me a pained look.

'You might've got away with it if you hadn't skipped at Gibraltar,' I said.

'No law against leaving your job, is there?' she said indignantly. 'They want to hang me for deserting the ship?'

'The faked references should prove intent to defraud,' I said. 'Actually the company's more interested in how it was done than anything else. You tell 'em how you got the references and how you got past their staff vetting and all the rest and they probably won't press charges. I don't think they'd like the publicity.'

'I don't know a bloody thing about all this,' she said angrily. She headed for the door. To Alias Coddington she said, 'You're a bloody mug, you are. You tell them what you like, I won't be in it.'

'Or I can scream for the law,' I said quietly, taking another gurgle at my can, 'if it gets to court I should think you're a cert for Holloway. It'll be easy enough to prove embezzlement, specially when we trace the other passenger.'

'What other bloody passenger?' she snapped. There's something frightening about a really angry woman I always think. Especially a good-looking one. You keep thinking you'd like to get a grip of her and that makes her hostility seem a lot more vicious.

178

Funny enough, I was embarrassed more than anything else. Of course I was earning out of it but I wasn't a policeman, I had no real right to be crashing into their lives like this. Tracking down Sidney Copeland the Dealer was one thing – he'd helped to put the mockers on Mrs Spencer's husband and she deserved help.

But now?

Uncle Sidney was only going along with me because he was scared rigid I'd shop him to Begg.

Now the two of us were going to con Jennifer Carmichael into coming clean about her card-sharping. A little tricky bastard and a big hard bastard scheming to get a lovely girl locked up? One to save his own neck, the other to get his hands on a slice of twelve hundred quid?

'Look,' I said, putting on a sympathetic face, 'they know you did two trips on the fiddle. You recruited Uncle – Simon here to help you and you dealt him near on five hundred quid's worth of winning cards. It won't be too difficult to find the geezer you recruited the trip before that. According to the computer you had it away with around fourteen hundred quid. The casino staff will remember which passenger did all the winning. If he's a respectable citizen he'll cough his guts when the bogeys get to him. I daresay you had to fake references because you'd already fallen foul of the law somewhere. That shouldn't be hard to dig up. So why don't you just do it my way?'

'Up yours,' she snapped. 'You can't prove any bloody thing. So a coupla punters had a lucky streak? And I happened to do a moonlight with one of them? Where does that get you? No bloody where.'

'Uncle Simon's going to come clean,' I said.

She glared at him. He twitched a bit.

'Yeah, sorry about that, Jen,' he said, looking everywhere else, 'only you know my position. If the law gives me a spin I'm sunk, in I?'

'You despicable old creep,' she shouted.

He looked at me for help.

I put a sneer on my face.

'How come a bonzer bird like you turned crooked in the first place – sport?' I said, as nastily as I could.

It was only to hide my embarrassment.

She was a prize and if only she'd had a drink with me that night in the ship's casino who knows where it would have led us.

She sat down and eyed me coldly.

I got up.

'I'm going to the carsi,' I said, 'don't dive out the window, cobber, cos Uncle Simon knows what'll happen to him if he lets you scarper. Okay, Uncle?'

He looked at me viciously.

I went up the stairs carrying the bag of money. It was a bathroom with real tiles on the floor and a glass shower cabinet. The bath and wash-basin and lavatory pan were in matching pink. I had a piss and a wash. I left the door open. I didn't think there was much danger of him letting her skedaddle but I wasn't under-estimating her. A quick bash on the bonce with a full whisky bottle was well within her range.

I dried my hands on a soft blue towel. I felt dead tired. In the cabinet mirror my eyes looked lifeless. I could've done with a bath in the big pink tub but I couldn't leave them alone too long.

Something had changed when I got back to the lounge. Uncle Sidney or Simon was guzzling into a whisky. She had a glass of something white, maybe gin, maybe just tonic. She didn't look so hostile.

I got ready for trouble.

First I went outside and tossed the bag of money and the four passports in the boot of the Stag. I dropped my suede coat on top of the carrier-bag and locked the boot. Then I opened the hood and removed the rotor arm.

When I looked up at the windows I couldn't see their faces but I was pretty sure they'd been clocking me.

I went back inside, locking the front door.

There wasn't much I could do about the windows.

It was a long night.

We watched the vision for a bit but Thursday isn't a good night on the box. Which one is? She did us a meal, fried eggs, fried bread, baked beans, grilled sausages, chips – the frozen kind. Just for a laugh I took Uncle Simon's plate and gave him mine before the first bite.

'Think I'd try to poison you?' she sneered.

'No – he got more chips.'

We went back into the lounge. He poured himself a big scotch. She had a gin. They both tried to get me at it but I stuck to a can of beer.

How did I know they didn't have a shooter tucked away somewhere?

Round about nine o'clock she was putting Andy Williams' albums on the stereo and Uncle Sidney was rabbiting away about everything.

'How about a game of cards?' I said with an evil smile. 'You could show me some tricks, cobber, I got nephews and nieces who need impressing'

'Okay,' she said, to my surprise.

She had nice brown hands. We sat round the low coffee table, one of those glass jobs with an old brown map of the world. The whole house was full of classy items like that. Andy Williams was a bit of a let-down but the two of them obviously knew what they liked.

She did a few shuffles. Each time she dealt us the same cards.

'You're a marvel wiv the boards, you are,' said Uncle Sidney. He gave me a wink. 'Can I try that one?'

He enjoyed kidding her along.

Then he did his three-card deal.

He had her fooled every time. Two cards in one hand, one in the other, a simple drop, a fairly slow switch-round – and she still couldn't pick the queen.

He bounced up and down on the edge of his chair. He gave me a look and then he said:

'Jennifer, I gotta own up, I –'

'I wouldn't do any more owning up than you can help, Uncle Simon,' I said quickly, guessing what he was going to tell her. 'Save it for tomorrow.'

'Nah, I wanna tell her,' he said.

Short of chinning him there wasn't much I could do. Maybe he'd been itching to tell her all along. Maybe it was just the whisky and his compulsion to entertain people. I knew he'd regret it.

'I ain't Simon Coddington,' he started, 'I'm really Sidney Copeland. I don't live in Essex and I ain't got a car business. In a million years you ain't gonna guess wot I really do. Go on – have a bash.'

She frowned. She looked at him and then at me. I kept a blank face.

'You're a fool,' I said to him. 'I thought Sidney Copeland was dead?'

Would he be told?

'Nah, Jen an' me's made for each ovver,' he said. He leaned across the glass table but couldn't lean far enough to kiss her. He squeezed her hand. 'I've waited for you all me life,' he said, his eyes big with love and gratitude.

'Tell me more,' she said brightly.

'You ain't gonna believe this – I wasn't ever gonna tell yer but we can't have any secrits from each ovver, can we? Know wot I really do for a livin'? I'm a street card-sharp, ain't I? King ov the three-carders, that's me. Yeah, straight up.'

She gave me a quick look.

'He'll bear me out, wonchyer, Jim? That's how he cottoned on to me, wunnit? Saw me workin' the boards in Oxford Street. Cor, that was a lark, he couldn't believe I was the same bloke as Simon Coddington on the ship, could yer, Jim?'

'So where did all the bread for this place come from?' she asked.

'Ah ha,' he said, wagging his little finger in front of his nose, 'that's dynamite that is.'

He got to his feet and kissed the top of her head. Then he moved over to the piano. He stood there, glass in his left hand,

right hand picking out notes. Now Is The Hour! At least that
was my guess.

'All my life I've wanted one of these,' he said, 'that's wot I
always fancied doin', wunnit, playin' the joanna? Charlie Kunz
– wunt he terrific? You don't remember him, Jen, do yer?' He
stabbed at the keys and then turned away from it. 'You gotta
learn it while yer young,' he said bitterly. He sat down again.
'So you wanna hear about it, Jen?'

I had to sit there while he told her the lot. Even down to the
bag of money in the boot of my car. The more surprised she
looked the better he liked it. He kept getting himself refills of
scotch. Maybe the strain had caught up with him at last. He
began to look old.

I went to the upstairs bathroom.

When I came back he was speaking in a new voice altogether.
Slightly slurred but, for once, from the heart.

'Yeah, ever since I was little I fancied bein' a piano player.
Fat chance. Eleven ov us, not half-a-dollar in the bleedin' house
one week to the next? We used to hang about pubs at night
lookin' after blokes' bikes for a ha'penny. Freezin' we was – an'
hungry? I was the ninth. If I tell you. Swear to God. My Mum
had eleven an' only six got to twelve year old. My old man went
on the missin' list when I was about five. Just left her to bring
us up best she could? Wot else was I gonna turn out but a
fakkin thief? Yeah – you two might not think it but in my head
I always noo I had creative leanin's, you know wot I mean?
The teachers said I was full ov *aptitude*. Yeah, that was the
actual word, *aptitude*. Slept five or six to a bed an' niver had a
decent pair ov shoes till I was sixteen, even then I hadda nick
'em. Yeah, nicked 'em out ov a shop in Bethnal Green Road . . .'
His eyes closed. Then he shook himself, wiping at his lap where
some whisky had spilled. 'Not bin a happy life. Vera? Met her
at a dance in Stratford, we was only about eighteen or that,
second time I give her one she gets in the bleedin' club. Love
her? Leave me out! Only wiv her family I didn't have no
option, did I? Right crowda villains them. Cripple yer quick as
look at yer.' He shook his head, fuzzy eyes staring into the

distance. 'I give 'em all them funny nicknames, din I? Desperate an' Bungalow an' all the ovvers. Know why? Cos they're horrible an' I'm tryin' to kid myself it's all down to coppin' a few quid an' havin' a lark an' a giggle. You couldn't tell none ov them you had creative leanin's – know what I mean? I once went to a concert in the Wigmore Hall, you believe that? Yeah, I told one ov them an' he told the whole world an' for years they fakkin called me Myra Hess. Remember her, she was a top pianist? Took the mickey outa me somethin' rotten they did. Yeah, brainless bastards.' He closed his eyes and shook his head and came up smiling. 'Only that's all behind now, innit?'

He let the glass drop on his lap but didn't seem to notice. All he knew was he loved her and they had plenty of money and tomorrow after they'd done what I wanted they would take off in a jet and head for a life of love in the sun.

Then he passed out.

'Help me get him up to bed,' she said.

'Sure.'

I got him over my shoulder and we went upstairs. He was no weight at all, seven or eight stone at most. Nothing to him, really, just his wits and his tongue and his lightning melodies.

I let him slide on to the big double-bed, a four-poster, brass, brand-new. She pulled off his shoes and unknotted his tie and let him lie there on the silk bedcover. His eyes were closed and his mouth was sagging. His face had started sweating. There was a dry part on his forehead. That was where the skin of the wig came down so that the join wouldn't be where you'd look for it.

'So now you know all about him,' I said to her across his body.

'Let's have a bloody drink,' was her verdict.

She said she would get me another can from the fridge. I took one of the big armchairs. She brought in the can and stood over me for a moment longer than necessary.

Then she went across to the drinks cupboard. I felt for the ring flap without looking at the can. She'd already opened it. I had it to my lips before I wondered about that. She was bending down, her back to me, her lovely beam end tight against the flared trousers.

I sniffed at the hole in the top of the can. It smelled like beer. Yet she hadn't bothered to open any of the others.

When she looked round I had the can up-ended into my mouth. My adam's apple did a lot of swallowing. She sat down on the big sofa with her glass. She looked far too young and soft for what she was. Too young and too lovely. She pulled her legs up on to the sofa. Her bare feet were brown and so were her ankles. Her thighs were tight against the thin wool. Her dark brown eyes watched my face.

I wiped my lips with the back of my hand.

'He thinks the world of you,' I said. 'Love at first sight, was it?'

She gave me a slow, secretive smile. Just looking at her made me feel big and hard. That's what good-looking women are for, isn't it, to remind you that you're a man?

I cannot tell a lie, I was tempted.

There was twelve hundred quid involved, sure enough, but it's the magic moments that make a life, isn't it, not last year's bank statement.

Her dark brown eyes kept watching me.

I lifted the can and let her see me swallowing the lot.

I licked my lips and then frowned.

'That tasted funny,' I said, looking at the can.

'Did it really, sport?' she said softly, still smiling.

'Yeah.' I blinked a bit, the way you do when you can't focus properly. She went on watching my face. I put my hand over my eyes. Then I looked up and gave her a full frontal of my teeth. I held the can out over the table. 'Good job I didn't actually drink it,' I said, pouring the beer into the water-jug. 'What did you put in it?'

'I didn't put anything in it,' she said, innocently. 'You must watch too many teevee movies.'

'That's true.' I got up. 'I'll get a new one from the kitchen – don't run away, will you?'

When I came back she was lying back against the cushions,

her legs stretched along the sofa. Like the man said, if all you can see is ankles suddenly ankles will turn you on.

I sat down again.

'Must've been a bit of a shock for you, finding out the truth about him,' I said chattily.

'Balls to him,' she said softly, balancing her glass on her stomach. 'As a capitalist he was bearable but as a small-time street grafter he's bad news. And some London gangster trying to kill him? I need him like I need bloody clap.' She twisted her head round on the cushions and looked at me. 'That time you asked me to have a drink on the ship – what was on your mind?'

'What do you think?'

The dark brown eyes smiled.

'Well? Here I am, having a drink with you . . .'

'You mean I've found the keys to your heart?' I patted my trouser pocket.

'I'm not wanted?'

She had the glass against her cheek. Her eyes never left mine.

'You're well-wanted, darlin',' I said with a disgusting leer, 'only on balance you're worth more to me in readies than in beddies. You like it? Readies and beddies?'

She went on staring but the dreamy smile had gone.

It was a long night but neither of us felt like a nap, funnily enough. Maybe she hadn't put anything in the beer, maybe she hadn't only wanted to get me close enough for a snatch at the car keys but I knew there was only one thought going on behind those dark brown eyes.

There was forty grand and her passport in the boot of my car and the keys were in my trouser pocket. She was lovely but she was as hard as the stony-hearted pavements of Oxford Street and I could see her scheming every minute of that long night. There was nothing she wasn't going to try to get hold of the loot in the boot.

We talked a lot. She told me how she'd gone crooked in the first place. She'd started out as an air hostess after leaving

186

school in Melbourne. That had been too much sweat for a sheilah with her brains. She'd then taken a croupier course. That had been more in her line but the wages weren't too clever and she'd decided early on what this life is all about.

'Most of these bunny girls are looking for millionaires,' she said, 'but you ever seen many millionaires? If they aren't ugly they're bloody boring. And the girls – well, they're mainly stupid cows with big boobs. It's a flesh-market. Was I going to stand there and wait for some fat little creep to crawl all over me? Not me, sport, I decided to grab my share without having to lie on my back for it. I was a top-class mechanic and the bread was there.'

'But you had to lie on your back, didn't you, to pick up blokes like Uncle Sidney?' I said. It was a bit brutal but now we were down to cases I wasn't seeing a soft, feminine lovely but a cold-hearted thief who happened to be in a beautiful body.

'I liked him,' she said indignantly, 'I wouldn't let any stray bastard screw me, you know.'

'So how did you tumble you were being watched?'

'That other bloke, Kevin? The string bean? He kept hanging about my table so I asked him if he wasn't supposed to keep a watch on the whole shooting-match and not just me. And he said in that drippy accent, I've been told to keep a special eye on you, cobber.'

'The stupid bastard.'

'He meant it as a joke, I think, but if you aim to stay alive in this racket you gotta be as cute as a shithouse rat. So I told Simon or whatever the hell he's called they were on to us and he said we'll skip. He had plenty of bread so I went along with him for the ride. He brought me here straight from the airport. He said it was a house he happened to own and I could stay as long as I wanted.'

'But you didn't fancy him all that strong?' I felt sorry for Uncle Sidney at that moment. Still, it was going to make it easier on my conscience when I turned her over in the morning.

'You joking? It was just a place to stay for a while till I got it all together again. He's good for a few laughs and he doesn't expect too much between the sheets.' She snorted with contempt. 'Not that he's capable of much.'

Suddenly my conscience was clear.

Poor old Uncle Siddenay.

We left the house at nine. I was unshaven. Uncle Sidney offered me a loan of his razor but that's something I could never do. Borrow a wife, yes, but never a razor. I replaced the rotor arm.

I told Jennifer to sit in the front passenger seat. Uncle Sidney got in the back. He looked very neat and prosperous in his good gear but his face was suffering.

'Done it all wrong last night, din I?' he said, groaning in the back seat. 'Legless, wun I? Was I givin' you two a lotta fantasy spiel by any chance? Cor, me north an' south is like a wrestler's jockstrap. Here, this gonna take long, Jim?'

'I dunno,' I said.

She didn't say anything. She was wearing a nice blue trouser-suit with those squared-toed leather shoes women thought were attractive that year. We arrived at Lombard Street about ten, not bad time considering the state of the traffic. It took about ten minutes to get parked. I unlocked the boot and lifted out the carrier-bag.

The lift took us to the cruise company offices on the sixth floor. I told the girl at the reception desk we were for Mr Barclay. She asked us to take a seat. None of us felt relaxed enough to take her up on it. Uncle Sidney kept soaping his hands and making unfunny comments on the people who came through the foyer.

It was one of those black leather and Muzak set-ups. They had a big display rack of their cruise brochures. I was thinking it would have been no great loss if I'd never heard of R. K. Brown and their rotten cruises.

Jennifer Carmichael was the calmest of the three of us. During the ten minutes Barclay kept us waiting she just stood there looking calm and lovely.

I reckoned she was planning on taking a powder as soon as

she got her passport out of me. She was welcome as far as I was concerned. Once I'd delivered them both to Barclay and they'd made their statements they were out of my hands.

The way I saw it then was that Barclay would call in the law. She was a cert for embezzlement.

Uncle Sidney?

I'd do my best for him. He was a crook in his own right but he'd been a bit unlucky falling in with her. Every time I looked at him I couldn't help marvelling. He'd seen his chance and dived straight in and then he'd kept the balls in the air. At fifty-three? I should have half his apple.

We were shown into the big boardroom. Mr Barclay had two other men with him. One was the company solicitor, a short, plump geezer with rimless specs, Mr Marley. The other was another director, one of those aristocratic types, exquisite tweeds and more good breeding than the royal stables. His name was Sir Oswald Stephenson. Proper Lord of the Manner he was. The way he got a chair pulled out from the big shiny table for Jennifer you'd have thought she was due for tiaras.

She kept a tight face and sat down.

Uncle Sidney gave me a pained look and took a chair farther up the big table on the other side.

Mr Barclay took the top place. I was sitting on his right. The carrier-bag was between my feet. He coughed politely. I put both elbows on the table. Sir Oswald offered his cigarette case all round. He gave Jennifer a charming smile. She just sat there with her hands folded on the table.

I wondered if she'd still be as cool when the roof caved in on her.

Which just proves that I wasn't really so clever after all. She'd already thought it all out. Nobody was cute enough to put her in the dock.

Chapter Eighteen

'Will you start the ball rolling, Mr Hazell?' said Barclay.

'Okay.' I swallowed but tried not to let anybody notice. It hadn't escaped me that this could be a big break for me. If I didn't blow it.

'My name's James Hazell,' I said, for the benefit of Marley and Sir Oswald. 'I was employed by Miss Wilmington's agency until a couple of weeks ago. I had the job of going on your boat the SS *Apollo* because Mr Barclay thought there could be a fiddle going on in the ship's casino. I was planted on the ship as a casino security man. Second night from Southampton Mr Coddington –' I nodded at Uncle Sidney – 'won four hundred and eighty quid playing blackjack at Miss Carmichael's table. I thought that might mean something so I kept a watch on her. I also asked Kevin Barclay –' I nodded at Mr Barclay. He smiled.

'My son was also attached to the casino,' he explained all round, sounding quite proud, 'he's doing the usual rounds of the company operations.'

Uncle Sidney breathed out and looked at the ceiling. Jennifer Carmichael frowned, leaning forward slightly.

'Unfortunately Miss Carmichael became aware she was being supervised more closely than usual and she decided to jump ship at Gibraltar,' I went on. 'She took Mr Coddington here with her – or vice versa. They've both told me the whole story. Miss Carmichael had worked this dodge on her previous trip. She found a suitable passenger and suggested she would deal him winning hands and then they would share the money. Mr Coddington agreed – a bit foolishly as he now realizes – and for reasons he'll probably tell you himself he didn't want to be the subject of any investigation. So then we checked and found that Miss Carmichael's references weren't kosher – I mean, they'd been faked on the notepaper of some London casinos and your company hadn't been too clever about checking up.'

'We've rectified that situation of course,' Barclay said to his mates. Marley the solicitor was making notes in a little black book. Even from there I could see how good his handwriting was.

'I came back from the voyage and then left Miss Wilmington's company,' I went on. 'I'm now in business on my own in Mayfair. During another enquiry I happened to catch sight of Mr Coddington and followed him to his home in Twickenham. Jennifer Carmichael was also living there. I was able to persuade them both to come here this morning to make a full statement to you gentlemen. I didn't promise them anything because I'd no authority but I did think it possible that if they came here voluntarily and owned up and paid back all the money nicked from the casino your company might not press charges. I think we're talking about something like fifteen hundred quid. Pounds. Near on five hundred that Mr Coddington had on his trip and around a thousand Miss Carmichael diverted the way of another passenger on the other trip. I don't know if she's willing to tell you the name of the other passenger but he shouldn't be too difficult to trace.'

I sat back.

The three R. K. Brown gents were looking a bit unsure of themselves. Maybe it was the first time they'd been face to face with the tricky lower orders. Barclay humphed enough to clear ten throats. Then he looked at Jennifer.

'You're willing to make a full admission and pay back the money?' he said.

She sat back in the big upholstered chair.

'Am I hell.' Her eyes were on me. 'First I'm admitting nothing, secondly I don't have any money to pay back and third I'm taking no part in any bloody kangaroo court.'

Consternation all round. Everybody looked at me. I looked at Uncle Sidney. He knew what I was telling him.

'Yeah well,' he said, 'wot Jim says is all kosher as far as I'm concerned an' I'll make you a full verbal. An' I'm willin' to pay back the gelt. I was a mug to fall for it – I mean, I didn't need the bunce, did I?'

'I see,' said Barclay. He looked at Marley, who nodded. 'I wonder if you would excuse us a moment?' He got up. The three of them went to the door. We were left alone, Jennifer, Uncle Sidney and I.

'You're only making trouble for yourself,' I said to her.

'Yeah – wot's the game?' demanded Uncle Sidney. 'Tell 'em the facts an' let's git the hell outa here.'

'Do what you bloody like,' she snapped.

Marley put his head round the door.

'Mr Hazell, could we have a word with you?'

I went outside leaving the two love-birds to snarl little nothings at each other.

They were having a conference in the next office.

'I thought you said they were both willing to make a full admission,' said Barclay.

'She seems to have changed her mind,' I said. 'But he's still game.'

'She was right in describing it as a kangaroo court,' said Marley nervously. 'My inclination is to turn the whole thing over to the police immediately. The company can't be seen to be pressurizing individuals into relinquishing their legal rights. If she was willing to confess and pay back that might be different but in view of what she said I don't think we've any alternative.'

'I'll agree with whatever you think is best, of course,' said Sir Oswald. 'Seems a pity though – always better to stay out of court, donchyou think?'

'On the other hand we must think of all the other casino staffs,' said Barclay. 'Shouldn't we shoot her pour encourager les autres?'

I can spell it now because I looked it up. At the time I thought he said poor ong cooradgay Les Oaters. Who Les was I didn't know. It was French, of course. Well, it took me long enough to get on top of English.

'Tell you what,' I said, 'let's tell her you're going to call in the law and see how that grabs her? Maybe she's counting on you being shy of publicity.'

'That sounds eminently sensible,' said Sir Oswald. Maybe it was just your aristo's natural gallantry. Maybe she'd got to him sitting there looking so lovely.

'If that's the general concensus,' said Barclay. 'Yes?'

We went back in. They were not talking to each other. We sat down.

'I'm afraid we now have no option but to call in the City of London police,' said Barclay.

Uncle Sidney gave a start. He glared at me.

'But you said –'

'Don't blame me,' I snapped back, looking at her.

She just sat tight.

'Very well then,' said Barclay. He pressed a buzzer on a black panel with a wire running under the table. The door opened. A middle-aged woman came into the big room. I sat back and stared at the panelled walls. Each panel carried a painting of a ship. Poor old Uncle Siddenay I thought, he's had it now.

'Miss Hennessey, I'd like you to –'

'Don't do anything rash,' interrupted Jennifer.

We all looked at her. Miss Hennessey stood there obediently.

'Is there something you want us to know?' Barclay asked her.

'Yes,' she said, looking at nobody in particular. She wasn't quite smiling but I knew she was enjoying herself. She looked down the room at Miss Hennessey and then at Barclay. He raised an eyebrow at Miss Hennessey and she left the room. Jennifer stared at a spot above my head. 'I've decided to give you a full statement.' We all nodded at each other. Prematurely.

'I admit everything,' she said. 'In fact, I'll tell you more than Hazell thinks he knows. I jumped the ship with him because I knew the security were on to me. The reason I knew was that your son Kevin told me. He was working with me on that trip. We were sleeping together from the second night out. He wanted a third of everything I was stealing.' She looked around all the faces.

193

'Not true,' I said to Barclay.

'It's a damnable lie,' he snapped at her.

'It's what I'm going to say in my statement and in the court and all the way to the bloody prison,' she said calmly. 'He'll deny it, natch, but who wouldn't? You can't prove he wasn't in my cabin and then it's just his word against mine.'

Uncle Sidney stared at her with wide open eyes. Then he looked at the others. Then he looked at me. He winked. He was proud of his lovely girl. Why the hell hadn't he thought of that?

The four of us went out for another confab. I felt a bit silly but that's what the big bosses wanted. This time there wasn't a lot to discuss. I told them I would bet my whole fee that Kevin had nothing to do with it but I couldn't prove it in court. There was no way Barclay was going to let his Kevin come in for all the shit she could stir up.

'So we just take a statement and the money from them and let 'em go?' I said, thinking that wouldn't be such a bad idea.

'I don't think the company should even get itself involved to that extent,' said Marley. 'My advice is that we should thank them for coming in and take no further action. If we take statements and money from them and she insists on naming young Mister Barclay in her statement we would be left vulnerable to a charge of conspiring to conceal a criminal offence – particularly if we'd taken back any money. No, I think we should wash our hands of the whole thing.'

'I think Marley's possibly right,' said Sir Oswald, 'after all we know now how she was swindling us and we'll know to be a lot more careful when we hire people in future.'

'I agree,' said Barclay.

'I don't mind,' I said, 'long as I get my fee. Not my fault they won't be convicted.'

'Our agreement was with Miss Wilmington,' said Barclay, 'however, I'm sure we can come to an arrangement.'

'I don't work for her now,' I said, 'I did all this under my own steam. I think you owe me at least six hundred pounds. Sorry to be stroppy about it but I've put a lot of work into this.'

Barclay gave me the bland look, the one that's supposed to tell underlings when to keep quiet.

Sir Oswald even patted me on the back.

'Good work,' he brayed, 'damned good show.'

'The company will no doubt see that you're adequately re-compensed through a purely ex gratia payment,' said Marley.

'Never mind ex gratia,' I snapped. 'That little bastard and her are going to walk off with fifteen hundred quid of your money. Even at six hundred I'm getting less for being straight than they are for being a couple of hooks! Six hundred is what I think fair. You going to pay me or do I have to sue you in the county court? You might win the case me not having a written agreement but it'll make good reading – specially with you letting them off scot free.'

They looked at each other. Sod 'em, I thought. Uncle Sidney had taught me that much. Doors don't stay open too long in this world so dive in while you can.

It won't make you popular, as I quickly discovered, but who wants to be a popular doormat?

'I object to your manner,' said Barclay, 'but we'll pay you. I'll tell Miss Hennessey to make out a cheque.'

'Thanks.'

We went back into the boardroom. Uncle Sidney was stand-ing beside Jennifer's chair, his hand on her shoulder. She was smiling at me.

'Well we want to express our thanks for your coming here this morning,' said Barclay, sounding a lot more friendly to them than to me, 'we've been extremely interested in what you've told us but we feel there's no further action we can use-fully take.'

'You mean that's it?' chirped Uncle Sidney.

'Thank you very much again.'

'Yes, indeed, been of great help to us,' neighed Sir Oswald.

Marley, without prejudice, said rhubarb rhubarb . . .

When the three of us came out on to the pavement Uncle Sidney did a little jig.

'You're a bleedin' wonder you are, mate,' he chirruped, giving her a kiss on the cheek. 'Wot a stroke to pull outa the bag? Wunnit triffick, Jim?'

'Here's your bloody money,' I said, shoving the carrier-bag in his chest.

'Dint they bung you a few quid then, Jim?' he asked, laughing like a drain. 'After all that sleuthin'? Cor, there ain't no justice, issair? Here – let Uncle Siddenay slip you a contribution.'

'I don't want none of Begg's money,' I growled. 'I got paid all right. Not a lot but at least I won't have to look over my shoulder for The Dentist every moment for the rest of my bloody life.'

He shuddered, stopping in mid-gurgle.

'Yeah, you're bleedin' right. Let's git the hell out ovvit, Jen.'

'The passports,' she said to me.

'They're in the bag. Have fun while you're running.'

I walked away from them.

'Hey, Jim-Jim?' Uncle Sidney's voice called after me, 'you couldn't see your way to drivin' us back to the house, could yer? No, you couldn't I expeck. Only them taxis are dead slow, inney?'

'You got a nerve,' I said.

But I drove them anyway. He was a hard bloke to stay angry at for long, the little dealer.

'How did you think up that brainwave ov draggin' in the boss's son?' Uncle Sidney asked her in the car.

'I suppose I'm like that,' she said, 'just devious by bloody nature.'

'You're the one for me, gel,' he exclaimed, taking hold of her hand through the gap in the front seats. 'You jealous ov me, Jim?'

'Greener than grass,' I growled.

I parked the Stag in the road. We went into the house, Uncle Sidney carrying the bag. She said she would pack. He phoned British Airways at Heathrow. There was a flight to Johannesburg at two p.m. It was about half-past eleven. He booked two seats, giving the names as Simon Coddington and Jennifer Carmichael. First-class, of course.

'Hope they don't catch you taking forty grand in cash out of the country,' I said.

'Nah,' he said, giving me the usual wink. He dived into a cupboard under the stairs. He came out with a big brown and white golf bag, brand new, full set of hooded clubs. He opened the carrier-bag and ripped off the brown paper. The money went down among the golf clubs, bundles of tens and twenties, brown money, a dream come true.

He zipped the bag.

'They won't look in a fakkin' golf bag I shouldn't think,' he chortled.

'They lose a lot of luggage,' I said.

'You see? You worry too much, Jim-Jim. Live dangerously for a change. It's the only way to prosper these days, me old son. Let's have a drop ov scotch. Jen! Hurry wiv the packin', we'll have a drink.'

'Coming,' she shouted back down the stairs.

Uncle Sidney and I had a scotch.

'Here's to your horrible good luck,' I said.

'Tell you wot,' he said, fishing in his jacket pocket, 'here's that bundle I copped from that woman wiv the dead husband, I don't fakkin need it, do I? Give it back to her – or bung it in yer own bin, I don't care, do I? I don't want to think you got nuffin out ovvit, Jim. You was very cliver you was. Go on – take it.'

'All right, I'll give it back to her,' I said, shoving Mrs Spencer's hundred and fifty into my jacket pocket.

'If it was me I'd hold on to it but you're the honest type,' he chirped.

She came down and we had another drink and then we went outside. She had two suitcases. He had the golf clubs and a leather holdall.

We put them into the boot of the Jensen.

'You want this car, Jim?' he said, seriously. 'I ain't takin' it wiv me an' I don't expeck to be back.'

'Bent is it?'

'Nah! Paid cash, din I? Six grand there, Jim, not a bad motor. He oughter have it, eh Jen?'

'Why not? He did his best to get us bloody locked up. You going to move the Scimitar so we can get the Jensen out?'

'Okay, sweetheart.' He looked at me. I remembered I had the keys. I held out both sets. He chucked the Jensen keys to her and did a little skip across the gravel.

He backed the Scimitar out of the gate.

She got into the Jensen and switched on. The engine burst into life like a supercharged fart. Was he serious about giving it to me? I wouldn't believe it till I had the keys and the log-book in my mitt.

Was I going to take it?

I didn't get a chance to find out.

She reversed the yellow gleam into the road. He drove the Scimitar in through the gate and into the garage. He came out and pulled down the door.

'We'll leave that one with the house,' he said over his shoulder to me, locking the garage door. 'You come wiv us in the Jensen to the airport then you can have it, Jim me old son. Now I'll just lock up the house and –'

The deep growl of the Jensen made us both look round at the road.

We had a quick glimpse of that unmistakable glass rear and then it was gone behind the big hedge. We both ran to the pavement. We got a quick glimpse of yellow as it disappeared round the corner.

'Wot's she doin'?' he squeaked.

I bent down and picked the blue passport off the pavement where she'd chucked it out of the Jensen window.

Then we both ran to the Stag.

I gave it hot licks but she had a two minute start. In that car? No chance.

I drove as far as the main road but she wasn't to be seen in either direction.

We sat there looking at the streams of cars and lorries and vans and caravans.

'She did leave you with your passport, give her that much,' I said, holding it out.

All he could say was:

'But she really loved me, I know she did.'

We went back to the house. We unlocked the front door and we went into the big lounge with the french windows. I got him a scotch. I didn't have anything.

'You could report it stolen,' I said.

'She knows I wouldn't chance it. Wiv forty grand in a golf bag?'

'I told you not to tell her about Begg and all that.'

'Yeah but we was in love, wun we?'

We heard a car but when we got to the front door it had passed. She wasn't coming back. He looked ready to weep. He was so small and perky and there he was, a broken man. I wasn't feeling too cheery myself. Sure he was a little rascal but that didn't put him out of the human race, did it?

Trust Uncle Sidney.

For ten minutes he stood staring out the french windows at the big, uncut lawn. I sat on the sofa and watched him.

'Well, when you flog this house you'll have about forty grand to come,' I said.

He pulled his left hand down his face, his head bent. Then he shook himself. He tossed over the rest of his whisky.

Next thing he was bouncing towards me, rubbing his hands together.

'Wot time was that fakking flight to Jo'burg? Two o'clock? Yeah – why not?'

'You got any loot?'

He started delving.

I brought out Mrs Spencer's hundred and fifty and threw it at him.

'That's a start,' he said, taking it as easily as he'd given it away. 'Now then – wot've we got here, me old son?' He started bringing out papers and general rubbish from the pockets of his mohair suit, unfolding creased notes of all denominations. 'Cor – that's a help,' he said, coming on a thicker bundle of fivers. 'That's the team's workin' capital, that is. I was the one Desperate trusted to hold it.' He laughed like a drain. 'Sorry about that, chaps.'

When all the notes were straightened and counted he had three hundred and fifteen quid. I said he could drive the Scimitar to a secondhand place and flog it but she'd taken the logbook. She'd also taken the deeds of the house. It was all in the luggage.

'Fakk her horrible luck,' he chirped, 'she can't flog it wivout me. I'll write to lawyers once I gits out there, they got copies of the deeds I expeck. Sod her the bitch. You couldn't drive me to the airport, no, you couldn't, could yer?'

So we drove to Heathrow and he bought a one-way ticket for the two p.m. flight to Johannesburg. It cost around two hundred and fifty. We went to the bar. I ordered two scotches while he counted the rest of his notes. He had about sixty quid.

He gave me a nudge and looked round the jet-set.

'Think we could buy a pack ov boards an' git a three-card school goin' in here?'

We both started to laugh.

When I stopped wheezing I felt in my hip-pocket. I was carrying fifteen quid.

'Here,' I said, pushing it in his handkerchief pocket, 'that'll give you a little extra when you get there.'

'That's handsome ov you, Jim,' he said.

We smiled at each other . . .

When they called the flight he patted my arm and straightened his jacket and gave me a wink. I went with him to the boarding gate.

'So what'll you do when you get there?' I said.

'I dunno, do I? Suss out the local action an' git in there I expeck. Don't you worry about me, me old son, gimme a

coupla weeks I'll either be a cannibal's breakfist or King ov
Africa, woan I?'

We shook hands.

'I don't know how you do it – at your age,' I said.

'Yeah well, anybody can lie down an' die, can't they, me old
son? See yer later I expeck.'

And off he went, to far-flung pavements.

It wasn't till I was sitting in the Stag in the airport carpark
that I realized I didn't have more than two bob in cash on me.
The tank was under half full. It was too late to run back and
tap Uncle Sidney for one of my pounds back.

Then I remembered Mrs Spencer, who owed me sixty quid.
I started her up and headed out of the airport.

On the way to Ruislip I stopped at a telephone box. The
phone had been vandalized but the S section was still intact in
the battered directory. I found the address for Arthur Spencer.

I got there about half-past two, thinking that Uncle Sidney
would probably be over France by then, provided the flight
took off on schedule.

I stopped having these nostalgic thoughts when I saw the
kind of houses I was passing. They weren't far short of bleeding
mansions!

The Spencer residence had a pokerwork nameplate by the
wrought-iron gate. *Helston Tor.* I parked the Stag and opened
the gate. It was a steep front garden, grass round rose-beds,
flower borders all over the shop. There was a middle-aged man
hoeing among the roses. He was well-dressed for a gardener,
suedes, cavalry twills, check shirt and Paisley cravat. Plus a
gold watch.

'Yes?' he said. A money voice.

'This where Mrs Spencer lives?' I said, looking up the paved
drive to the big house.

'That's right. Is she expecting you?'

'My name's Hazell, is she in?'

'I don't actually think so –'

We both looked together as she came round the corner of the house carrying a flat basket of flowers. She was in blue slacks and a blouse, a silk headscarf tied under her chin.

I walked up the paved drive towards her. It was a two-storey house with a glass conservatory running the length of one side. Detached. Big windows. I don't study the house market but I wouldn't have thought sixty grand was far out.

'Oh, it's you,' she said, blinking in the sun. She didn't look half so dreary as I remembered her.

'Yeah,' I said, looking over the house. 'I was out this way and I thought I'd drop in and settle our business. Nice place you got here.'

'Oh yes, of course there's an awful lot needs doing to it.'

'Everything all right, Susan?' called the good gardening friend.

'Yes, it's all right, George,' she called back. To me she said, 'I owe you sixty pounds, don't I? If you'll just wait here I'll get you a cheque.'

'Could you make a couple of quid of it in cash?' I said, 'only I've come out without any money and I'm strapped for petrol to get back to town. I'd be obliged.'

'I'll see, I'm not sure if we have any cash.'

I stood there in the sun watching him scratch the good earth. Then she came back with a cheque for fifty-five pounds and a fiver.

'Will you be wanting a receipt?' I asked her.

'I shouldn't think that would be necessary.'

'Right then.' I looked up and down the house again. Then I looked at her.

Of course I'd been conned.

Cut-rate work for the poor widow?

No wonder she'd been keen for me not to visit.

'Just out of interest,' I said, putting away the cheque and the fiver, 'what was the insurance worth in the end?'

Give her credit, she did smile.

But she didn't tell me.

None of my business, was it?

Chapter Nineteen

I never did hear again from Uncle Sidney. A few months later the papers were full of Billy Bunter Begg's trial for attempted murder, grievous bodily harm, extortion, wounding and conspiracy to defraud. He got twenty years. The Dentist got off lightly with fifteen. The judge recommended that they should never become eligible for parole.

I was nipping down Oxford Street the other day when I saw a three-card team at it. First off I spotted a dog-eye. You can't miss a bloke whose two eyes can look four different ways at once, can you?

Of course they've brightened up Oxford Street a lot since I did my big walk on Uncle Sidney's trail. They've banned private cars and widened the pavements. They've even bunged down seats and trees in big concrete pots.

This bunch of three-carders was working a pitch between Marble Arch and Quebec Street. The dealer was a burly young bloke with a Sinatra haircut and freckles. The moody four were just what you'd expect, a crombie coat, a drape jacket, a muffler.

As I passed they were geeing up the mug who'd nominated himself for dry-cleaning.

Different faces but the same routine. Different faces right enough – I'd have bet a year's readies that not one of them had the magic spark to juggle three separate identities the way the Old Master had.

Hardly a day passes but I don't wonder how he's getting on in Africa.

Mind you, I'm not always a good judge of people. Like Christine Bunn, for instance!

I'd only slowed down for a couple of paces but some bloke bumped into me from the back and then growled at me to watch where I was bloody going.

'Where's your white stick?' I snapped.

'Bloody wanker, get stuffed,' he snarled back, over his rapidly retreating shoulder.

I might have jobbed him but you could be fighting all day if you were keen enough, couldn't you?

Oh yeah, a lot's changed but it'll take more than trees in pots to soften that old stony heart.

More about Penguins and Pelicans

Elizabeth Ferrars in Penguins

The Small World of Murder

The invitation was too good to refuse: Christmas in Australia
with rich friends – and all expenses paid. But Nina has her
doubts as she travels around the world with Jocelyn and
Nicola Foley. Jocelyn and Nicola are trying to put their lives
back together again after the kidnapping of their three-
month-old baby. Or are they? And is someone trying to kill
Nicola? Or are her unfortunate accidents being caused by her
own unbalanced mind? These are the questions that haunt
Nina. In a search that takes her straight into the small world
of murder, Nina eventually finds the reasons behind Nicola's
accidents – but only after death has claimed several more
victims.

Breath of Suspicion

'Another masterpiece of craftsmanship from Miss Ferrars, a
professional down to her fingertips, who knows how to keep
you intrigued right up to the end. One scientist kills himself at
a secret research station in Sutherland and his partner
disappears. The trail leads to a sunny village in Madeira
where the breath of suspicion turns into a storm. A mystery
to test the most exacting mind' – *Northern Evening Despatch*

P. B. Yuill

Introducing James Hazell – 'the biggest bastard who ever pushed your bell-button . . .'

Hazell Plays Solomon

Inquiry agent James Hazell was a tough nut – an ex-copper from Bethnal Green, and newly cured gin disposal unit. Tug-of-war babies were not exactly his line. And this was going to be one mother of a case.

Compared with Hazell, Solomon had it easy. All he had to do was make up his mind. He never had a mobster with a shotgun threatening to blow his f------ head off.

Hazell and the Menacing Jester

'Splendidly real London shamus investigates wholly likely sub-world trickery. Real two-sided people, savoursomely sharp descriptions, an undertow of moral comment. First class' – H. R. F. Keating in *The Times*

'Hazell is a first-rate English private eye – tough, very witty, hard-working and obstinate . . . The plot is tense and absorbing' – *Bolton Evening News*

'Plenty of action, racy dialogue, and neat twist in the tail' – *Manchester Evening News*